THE ROMULAN THREAT CLOSES IN....

ZAR!

Spock felt an irrational impulse—to comfort his son. He reached out a hand, shook his shoulder gently. "Stop it, Zar."

Zar gasped, then ignored him. "I'm scared. I hate them. I'm going to die. . . . Die. . . ." His body stiffened, then the clenched hands loosened, and he tumbled over. . . .

Shocked, Spock stared at him. He went to the limp figure. He pulled his son's head into his lap, felt his throat—a flutter, very slight. . . . His fingers went to the temples. . . . Probing, reaching, calling desperately the name, over and over. . . . Zar! Zar! Finally. . . . Zar!

YESTERDAY'S SON

A.C. CRISPIN

A STAR TREK® NOVEL

PUBLISHED BY POCKET BOOKS NEW YORK

Another *Original* publication of POCKET BOOKS

POCKET BOOKS, a division of Simon & Schuster, Inc.
1230 Avenue of the Americas, New York, N.Y. 10020

ISBN: 0-671-60550-X

First Pocket Books printing August 1983

10 9 8 7 6

POCKET and colophon are registered trademarks
of Simon & Schuster, Inc.

STAR TREK is a Trademark of Paramount Pictures Corporation
Registered in the U.S. Patent and Trademark Office.

Printed in the U.S.A.

Dedicated to my two wonderful grandmothers,
with thanks for a lifetime of love and kindness;
and to my own son, Jason Paul Crispin

ACKNOWLEDGMENTS

I've always wanted to look at the acknowledgments page of a book someday and read: "I did it *all* myself!" But I couldn't say that here, because I owe many people thanks for their help in completing and marketing *Yesterday's Son*.

For their help in writing, editing, and proofing, my thanks to:

Debby Marshall, the best friend a writer ever had . . .

O'Malley, the Red Queen, ("Who *cares*, Ann? *Nobody* cares about a dumb detail like that; it doesn't advance the *story*. Out! Off with its head!"), who is a terrific editor—but don't ask her to spell . . .

Hope and George Tickell, my mother and father, who proofed and photocopied . . .

Faith E. Treadwell, my sister, who read and commented . . .

Jamie and Norman Jette, for the lesson in physics . . .

Sam R. Covington, for teaching me the value of research . . .

Robert B. and I. Lois Pleas, for well-considered comments on a stranger's work . . .

Beverly Volker, a fine editor, and a good person to Contact . . .

Randy L. Crispin, my husband, for giving me a reason to write . . .

Delma Frankel, that "deadeye" proofreader who turned out to be full of surprises . . .

And, for moral support and encouragement during the long years of uncertainty:

Andre Norton, who has enchanted so many people with uncountable wonders . . .

Jacqueline Lichtenberg, not only a good writer, but also a kind and gracious person who goes out of her way to help others get a start . . .

Anne Moroz, who finally found a safe place . . .

Teresa L. Bigbee, who puts up with writers and their attendant insanity with good grace, a sense of humor, and many helpful comments and suggestions . . .

Mary M. Schmidt, and Lynxie, of course . . .

Howard Weinstein, amateur psychotherapist, but truly a pro writer . . .

John McCall, professional fiction consultant, and a good one . . .

And, finally, a special acknowledgment to Shoshana (Susie) Hathaway, for giving me the idea, a long time ago, in a newly rediscovered Universe . . .

Introduction
Yesterday's Son

In the Author's Notes to my own STAR TREK novel, *The Covenant of the Crown,* I mentioned that I've made quite a few friends through STAR TREK, many of whom also want to be writers.

Ann Crispin is one of those friends, and *Yesterday's Son,* her first book, is a monument to patience.

I met Ann at the 1979 August Party Convention near Washington, D.C., where I'd unveiled the just-completed *Covenant* by reading chapters to audiences. Ann was *verrrry* pregnant at the time, and I think we bumped into each other (figuratively . . . or *was* it literally?) in the typically crowded, incredibly slow convention elevator.

I really don't recall exactly what we talked about—that's no reflection on Ann, just the fact that much of my time at conventions is spent talking about writing. Many fans are excellent writers, trying to build up the nerve to submit their work professionally.

I'm not a parent, but I'd imagine that sending out your first would-be pro story is even worse than sending your child to the first day of kindergarten. After all, most kids survive their first day of school—very few get mailed back with rejection slips. But most first stories *do* meet that ignominious fate.

And so it is that many writers never get up the gumption to take that risk. By the time we met in the elevator, Ann had already submitted *Yesterday's Son* and, not having heard a word from Pocket

Books, was getting anxious. Ann tells me she "hassled" me "rudely" for encouraging fans to try their hands at pro writing, insisting that previously unpublished writers wouldn't get the time of day from big time publishers and editors.

It is with a great sigh of relief that I blow Ann a big Bronx cheer and say, "I told you so!"

Not that *everyone* can do what Ann has done—scoring with her first-ever pro submission. I like to share my own writing experiences, offering what happened in my pursuit of this odd excuse for a career as an example. I was lucky enough to sell *The Pirates of Orion* to the animated STAR TREK TV series when I was 19 years old . . . and then I didn't sell anything for five years . . . five very sobering years.

So I'm no superstar writer. But I had a large enough ego to think I could tell stories well enough for other people to want to pay to read them. *And I could sell a story, maybe other semi-egotistical wishful thinkers can, too.*

That's probably what I told Ann, and she listened—poor fool! She thought about it for a while, then called me several months later to talk some more. And called a few months after that . . . and a few months after that . . .

At that stage, I should point out, our commiseration had become mutual. While Ann was grinding her teeth and awaiting the life-or-death final word on her manuscript, I was going through seemingly endless delays in the publication of my already-purchased-and-paid-for STAR TREK book. Long-distance phone calls aren't cheap, but they're usually cheaper than psychiatry, so I figure I saved Ann a lot of money over those next couple of years.

And both our vigils had happy endings. *Covenant* came out in December 1981, and has been very well received. Several months after that, Ann got the word from Pocket Books—*Yesterday's Son* was "go for launch!"

In July 1982, Ann sent me a manuscript copy to read. After the first two chapters, I knew it was a winner. The rest of the book did not let me down. And I was convinced it should have its coming-out as my book did, having chapters read at a convention.

Quite frankly, Ann was chicken. She didn't think she should read it because no one would be able to hear the words over the racket caused by her chattering teeth. Secretly, I was glad—because that meant I would have the distinct pleasure of reading those opening chapters to a packed ballroom at Summer Media Fest '82 in Arlington, Virginia.

That audience loved what they heard, but you are far luckier than they were . . . for *you* get to read the whole book, and you'll be glad you did!

Howard Weinstein
September 1982

P.S. If you write to Ann c/o Pocket Books, and you'd like an answer from her, please be sure to enclose a stamped, self-addressed envelope. New authors aren't rich enough to afford hundreds of return-postage stamps!

Prologue

Doctor McCoy picked up his rook and plunked it down again, taking one of his opponent's pawns. "Get out of that one if you can," he said, sitting back confidently. The man on the other side of the chessboard raised a quizzical eyebrow.

"An interesting move . . ." Spock conceded, and lapsed into an unmoving study of the board.

McCoy smiled. Spock had agreed to a game of the old-fashioned, two-dimensional chess when the Doctor suggested it. Now the Vulcan was discovering that McCoy's moves, though occasionally erratic, could be inspired, and a challenge to his logical mind. McCoy hadn't been captain of the chess team in med school for nothing.

While the First Officer mulled over his Queen's predicament, McCoy glanced idly around the recreation room. It was filled with crew members reading, playing cards or chess, or talking in groups. His gaze stopped on the face of a pretty young Ensign. The Doctor searched his mind for her name, recalled it. Teresa McNair. Straight out of the Academy, barely a day over twenty-three. Nice brown hair, green eyes. She had her nose in a micro-reader, scanning the material with careful scrutiny. As he watched, enjoying the long, slender legs curled up underneath her, she stopped the reader with a quick gesture and sat up. Tearing off two long strips of readout paper, she got up and walked straight toward him.

McCoy gave a guilty start, realizing he'd been staring, and turned away. A moment later, McNair appeared at Spock's elbow. "Excuse me, Mr. Spock."

The First Officer looked up. "Yes, Ensign?"

"Sir, would you please confirm a fact for me? I thought it was well-established that early Vulcan colonization was confined to the area closest to the Romulan Neutral Zone?" McNair's voice rose, making it a question.

"That's correct, Ensign." Spock was patience itself, but hardly inviting.

"Then do you know of any explanation for this?" She placed the large readout in front of the Vulcan and continued, "This photo came from archeological data published about the Beta Niobe system. That's clear at the other end of the explored portion of the Galaxy, and if there was no Vulcan colonization . . ." McNair sounded puzzled as she trailed off.

McCoy saw something flicker across Spock's face at the mention of Beta Niobe. He vainly tried to place it . . . no use, too many planets, too many suns. You had to be a biological computer like the Vulcan to remember half of them.

Spock scanned the sheet, eyes narrowed. The Doctor looked up at McNair. "Beta Niobe? Can't place it, but it sounds familiar."

The Ensign grinned at him and responded, "It should, Doctor. The *Enterprise* was the ship detailed to warn the people of Sarpeidon that Beta Niobe was ready to nova. I believe you were one of the landing party. There was a huge library complex on the planet. Our computers scanned and recorded the information in it before Sarpeidon was destroyed. The archeological information I was studying came right out of the Atoz Library." She turned back to Spock, who was still studying the readout. "Neutron dating places the cave paintings you can see as circa 5,000 years old—Sarpeidon's last ice age. This is an enlargement of the face you can see on the left." She spread another sheet in front of the First Officer.

14

Spock leaned forward, face a carven mask, and McCoy was alerted by his complete withdrawal. The Doctor edged around in his seat to study the photos.

The one nearest him showed a cave wall, gray, with reddish highlights. The first painting was a hunting scene. Two figures—humanoid—faced two large creatures. One looked like a lion with a skinny neck and long fur. The other stood on its hind legs, and resembled a bear that had been made to order by a committee. Floppy ears, long snout—it should have looked comical, but not with a mouthful of tusks, and a height nearly twice that of the hunters.

On the far left side of the wall there was another, smaller painting of a single face. McCoy craned his neck to see the other photo, the blowup of that face.

Glowing ghostly white against the dark stone of the cave wall, it seemed to float in front of the Doctor's incredulous eyes. Two slanting eyes, a jagged lock of bushy dark hair, a nose, a mouth. The style was primitive but arresting, and the features were executed with meticulous care. Including the pointed ears.

McCoy looked at Spock, whose expression was more remote then ever. The Doctor's mouth was dry, and his voice cracked on the words. "Sarpeidon? It's been two years since we . . ." He trailed off and sat back, biting his lip. Spock turned to McNair.

"Perhaps a genetic anomaly, or racial offshoot with interesting parallel development. Or, possibly, a representation of some mythical being. Remember Pan, from Terran folklore. I'd appreciate it if you'd allow me to look at that tape when you're finished, Ensign." The Vulcan's voice was completely normal. McNair nodded and left, taking the readouts with her.

Spock turned back to his chess partner. "If you don't mind, Doctor, I should like to return to our game, as I go on duty in forty-five point three minutes. I've thought of a way to negate your interesting, but illogical campaign."

McCoy's eyes narrowed. "It's your move, Spock. Or had you forgotten?"

The Vulcan barely glanced at the board, as he quickly moved a bishop. The Doctor didn't miss the tremor, immediately stilled, in the lean fingers.

McCoy took the hint, and pulled his chair back around. "Never doubted you'd beat me for a moment, Spock. All that logic has got to be good for *something.*"

But McCoy won the game.

Chapter I

Captain's Personal Log Stardate 6324.09

"Our current assignment of charting Sector 70.2 of this unexplored quadrant has been proceeding uneventfully—so uneventfully that I've been resorting to simulated battle drills and abandon-ship exercises to keep up my crew's efficiency. Everyone is looking forward to our scheduled inspection and repair detail at Star Base 11, and most of the crew have requested leave. Morale is high—partially because of the party planned for the evening we dock. The only members of my crew who aren't space happy are my Chief Medical Officer and my First Officer. Both have been remarkably quiet for the past two days. I haven't questioned either of them, but I intend to if this behavior continues."

The *Enterprise,* starship of the heavy cruiser class, glided serenely through space, unmindful of the excitement caused by her approaching overhaul at Star Base 11. Most of the crew, however, were polishing up assorted skills for the party. Lieutenant Sulu and Yeoman Phillips were giving an exhibition of fencing. The choral group was rehearsing some slightly raunchy—and slightly true—ballads about the Captain. (He was carefully remaining unaware of them.)

And the Little Theatre was staging *H.M.S. Pinafore.* The production was directed by Lieutenant Uhura, and Chief Engineer Scott, who had a fine baritone, was singing the part of Captain Corcoran. Kirk, Scotty and Uhura were discussing the operetta one afternoon at lunch, when McCoy joined them.

"Have a seat, Bones." Kirk took a determined bite from a large green salad and sipped his skim milk. "I'm going to turn into a rabbit if you keep putting me on these diets. And then I have to watch while Scotty gorges himself on Black Forest cake!"

The Chief Engineer swallowed and grinned. "A man's got t' keep up his strength if he's going t' work all day and then rehearse all night!"

"Actually, Captain," Uhura said, tapping a manicured nail thoughtfully against her dark cheek, "we ought to update the production a bit, don't you think? Rewrite Gilbert and Sullivan to make it more . . . contemporary. For instance, why not set the operetta aboard the *Enterprise,* and rename it? *U.S.S. Enterprise* has just as much ring as *H.M.S. Pinafore.* And then *you* could sing the Captain's part!"

Kirk chuckled, hummed a few bars, then broke into song. "And I'm never ever sick in space . . ." he warbled, innocent of key. Uhura and Scotty chimed in.

"What, never?"

"No, never!"

"What, *never?*"

Well . . . hardly ever . . ." Kirk broke off and grinned at McCoy. "What about it, Bones? Have I got a future in the opera? The singing idol of Star Fleet, huh?"

McCoy rolled his eyes. "In my professional opinion, you should've had your larynx removed at birth to prevent that possibility. As a starship Captain you'll get by. As a singer . . . sorry, Jim."

Kirk shook his head ruefully. "Another great career, nipped in the bud by lack of encouragement." He glanced at the chrono, stood up. "Got to get back to the bridge. Coming, Doctor?"

When they reached the relative privacy of the corridor, he asked casually, "What's up, Bones?"

McCoy shook his head and didn't answer. Instead he asked, "Do you remember a planet Sarpeidon we visited two years ago?"

The Captain gave him a sharp glance. "It took me weeks to get the smell of that medieval jail out of my nose. And that crazy old Mr. Atoz . . . What about it?"

Again the Doctor didn't answer. After a long pause, he queried, "Did Spock ever talk to you about what happened to us back there?"

"No, as I recall, both of you were pretty quiet about the whole experience. From the official report you logged, I gathered there was a woman back in that ice age who saved your lives. What was her name?"

McCoy hesitated. "Zarabeth. Have you seen Spock lately?"

"No. Should I have? He's been off-duty for the past 36 hours." Hazel eyes scanned the Doctor's face, concerned. "Sure you can't talk about it?"

McCoy avoided the steady gaze. "Nothing to talk about, Captain. I'll see you later."

Kirk stared at the empty corridor, tempted to follow and pursue the subject, but finally continued on his way. McCoy might not care to admit it, but he shared a certain kinship with Spock. If he didn't want to talk, he couldn't be persuaded.

The bridge was quiet and reassuring. Kirk dropped into his command chair, scanning the clipboard of reports, but one part of his mind was counting the minutes until Spock appeared for duty. The best First Officer in the fleet . . . yes, he was that, for sure. What could McCoy have been hinting at, harking back to Sarpeidon? And that woman? Was he talking about himself? Somehow, Kirk thought not. But Spock wouldn't get mixed up with a woman . . . at least he never had, except for Omicron Ceti III, and those spores . . . funny, he'd always thought there was something besides the damned spores working

on the Vulcan . . . and of course, there was T'Pring
. . . but that was different. . . .

The Captain jerked to attention, mind racing. It
was 1301, and Spock was one minute late for duty.
Impossible! But the computer tie-in flashed confirmation beneath his fingers.

Behind Kirk, the bridge door hissed shut, and
Spock was standing by the command chair, hands
clasped behind his back.

"Mr. Spock, is anything wrong? You're late." The
Captain's voice was quiet, concerned.

"I regret my tardiness, sir. It won't happen again."
The Vulcan's eyes were distant as they fixed themselves on a point three centimeters above Kirk's left
eyebrow.

Sighing inwardly, the Captain gave up, knowing
from long experience that Spock would talk when he
was ready—if ever. He stood up and said formally,
"You have the con, Mr. Spock. I'm due for an inspection of the hydroponics lab at 0815. Report anything unusual. This sector has been charted as having
some good-sized radiation storms."

The Captain left the bridge, aware of a nagging
prickle of disquiet at the back of his neck. Spock
would have called it illogical—Kirk called it a hunch.

Kirk continued to worry during the next three days,
as Spock's and McCoy's silence continued. He took
out his frustrations on the training android in the self-defense section of the gym.

He was relaxing in his cabin after one particularly
strenuous workout, sprawled facedown across his
bunk, reading. The volume was one of Kirk's own
cherished bound books. "The kind of book you can
hold in your hands," as Sam Cogley had put it. The
lawyer had introduced him to the hobby of collecting
"real" books, and Kirk had found this remarkably
well-preserved copy of an old favorite in an antique
shop on Canopus IV. He was absorbed in the ad-

ventures of Captain Nemo and the *Nautilus* when the door signal flashed.

"Come in," Kirk put the book back into its protective cover when the door slid open to reveal his First Officer. He waved an arm invitingly at a chair. "Sit down. Would you like some Saurian brandy?"

Spock shook his head at the brandy bottle, and Kirk poured a small shot for himself. He sat down opposite the Vulcan, cradling the snifter in his hands, and waited.

Spock hesitated for a long moment. "You've been expecting to see me."

The Captain nodded. When the Vulcan didn't continue, he said, "I've known something is wrong for several days. First McCoy clammed up, then you. I can tell it's serious. Want to talk about it?"

Spock looked away, absorbed in a painting of the *Enterprise* that hung on the opposite wall. Kirk had to strain to hear him. "I must request leave for an indeterminate amount of time. It is . . . a family matter."

The Captain took a slow sip of the brandy, and studied his friend. The Vulcan looked tired; there were new lines around his eyes, and an aura of disquiet had replaced the usual calm control. Kirk listened intently, waiting for Spock's next words, and was suddenly conscious of something subliminal seeping into his mind, touching, and for a moment he was feeling deep resolution, mixed with guilt and shame. He held his breath, trying to look inward, to focus . . . and the contact, if contact it was, and not his imagination, was gone.

Spock was staring at him. "Jim—you're not telepathic, I know, but for a moment—"

"I know. I felt it too—for a moment. Long enough to know that you're determined to go, and that the situation, whatever it is, is pretty bad. But you're going to have to tell me the rest in words, Spock."

"If I could, I would share this with you, Jim. But

I am responsible for this . . . problem. I must solve it alone."

"Something tells me that you're going to attempt something really hazardous. Am I right?"

Spock looked down at his hands, repeated, "I must go alone. Please don't ask me to explain why."

Kirk leaned forward, gripped the Vulcan's shoulder, and shook it. "I don't know what the problem is, but I know why you won't tell me. You're concerned that if I find out how dangerous this project is, I'll insist on going with you. You're right. I am."

The First Officer shook his head, and his voice was hard. "I will not allow it. I can't take the responsibility for your life, too. I am going alone."

Kirk set the snifter down with a thump. "Dammit, Spock, you don't have to tell me anything if you don't want to, but you'll have to desert to get off this ship without me."

Spock's jaw tightened, and his eyes held anger. Kirk stared into those eyes unflinching, and wondered where in hell Spock was going. Obviously, McCoy knew more than he was telling—*Sarpeidon? But that planet doesn't exist in the present. It blew up. The present . . . and the past . . . the woman . . . and the face on the wall of the cave . . . Cave? Face?*

Kirk straightened. The image in his mind was clear—a Vulcan face painted on a cave wall—nothing he'd ever seen before. "I got it that time, Spock. Call it empathy, telepathy, what you will, I know, now. This has to do with . . . biology, doesn't it?"

The Vulcan nodded mutely, then leaned his head in his hands. His voice was strained. "Yes. My barriers must be slipping, if I could broadcast that loudly. Of course, we've been mind-linked, but . . . I'm tired, that must be it. . . ."

"Never mind the explanations. I know, and it doesn't matter how." Kirk looked at the Vulcan and breathed, "It's incredible . . . 5,000 years ago in that frozen hell . . ."

"Zarabeth bore my child." Spock finished for him.

They stared at each other for a long moment, and finally the Captain stirred. "Maybe there's another explanation. Maybe Zarabeth painted *you*. You can't be sure. . . ."

"I am sure. The face on the wall shows unmistakable Vulcan characteristics, but it's not my face. The eyes are different. The hair is longer. The features are those of an adolescent, or not much older. There are other things. The artifacts found in the cave along with the paintings show a higher level of civilization than the evolving race in that hemisphere had yet achieved. Traces of worked metal—a stone lamp that used animal fat. Anachronisms in that time period."

Kirk was convinced, but shook his head. "Tormenting yourself over a child that lived and died 5,000 years ago doesn't make sense. There's nothing you can do about it."

Spock looked at him calmly. "I am going back to get him."

The Captain didn't know what he'd been expecting, but it wasn't this. "But . . . Spock . . . *how?*" Even as he said the words, a sudden, still-painful memory bit at him. "All is as it once was . . . let me be your gateway. . . ." He took another swallow and felt the brandy burn his throat. "The Guardian of Forever, you're going to use it to go back."

The Vulcan nodded.

"Spock, that planet's been declared off-limits, except for the archeological expedition. They won't let you get near it, let alone go through. To get permission to use the Guardian would take a lot of clout—probably by someone the rank of a planetary governor, at least. . . ." He thought for a second, then answered himself again. "T'Pau."

"A logical deduction, Captain."

Kirk thought of T'Pau, tiny, frail, ancient . . . but packing enough authority in one request to override a Star Fleet Admiral's orders. Yes, she had the clout, all right. Would she use it?

Kirk said as much. The First Officer looked grim. "She will intercede, when I tell her the reason. The family is all-important on Vulcan. Family loyalties overrule even planetary law. Vulcan is virtually governed by an oligarchy composed of several prominent families. Mine is one of them. And T'Pau will not let one of the family live and die alone, far from his people."

"I don't envy you your mission, Spock," the Captain shook his head. "I wouldn't want to have to explain this to her."

"I am not looking forward to it, I assure you. But it must be done. It's my duty." Spock stood up, hesitated. "I assume that my request for leave can be approved immediately? We can divert to Andros in the Antares system with a loss of only one hour and thirty-two point four minutes."

Kirk nodded and got to his feet. "It's settled. I'll have your leave request processed immediately. If we drop you off on Andros, you should be about a week getting to Vulcan. . . . Getting clearance and returning to Star Base 11 should take you about another ten days. Good thing we've got that overhaul coming up. . . . Yes, that'll work . . . I'll be ready to go when you return. With luck, we'll be back before the final inspection is finished. Well? What are you standing there for?"

"Captain, I must go alone—I absolutely refuse—"

Kirk cut him off in mid-sentence. "It's settled. Blackmail, Mr. Spock. I don't go, you don't get leave. Simple as that."

"This could be hazardous. . . . I can't allow you to risk . . ."

"Quit arguing. And quit trying to wrap me in cotton. Humans may not be as strong as Vulcans, but that doesn't give you a right to tell me what I can and can't do. After all, who's in command here?" Kirk glanced at the chrono. "You've got forty-five minutes to get ready. I'll see you in two and a half weeks. Move!"

Spock found that he'd responded to the snap of that last order automatically, and was standing in the corridor looking at a closed door. He shook his head ruefully, and hurried off to pack.

Chapter II

Midday on Vulcan. The heat swirled around Spock as he materialized on the crest of a ridge, and he stood soaking it in for a moment, sniffing appreciatively at the thin air. Its dryness felt wonderful after the cold fog that passed for atmosphere aboard the transport freighter. Overhead, the sky flamed as 40 Eridani reached its zenith. The white sand reflected the heat back in a searing glare, and the rocks and vegetation shimmered.

Spock skirted the low, sprawling building, heading for the visitor's entrance on the south side of the living complex. He didn't intend to announce his arrival, though it had been more than a year since he'd since his parents. He felt a twinge of guilt, visualizing their disappointment if they discovered his visit; repressed it. Amanda would want to know the reason for his sudden arrival, and how long he was going to stay, and Sarek would expect him to tour the estates. He'd be swamped with family duties, and there would be questions. . . .

Inside, he keyed his request for an audience with T'Pau, then waited impatiently, forcing calmness over his features, curbing his body to stillness. Finally the screen beside him lighted with the characters of his first name, the one used only by family, and then only on name-days and religious holidays. He'd used it deliberately, knowing T'Pau would recognize its import, and respect his request for privacy. Directed to one of the clandestine inner passages that led to T'Pau's sitting room, he threaded the narrow darkness quickly, then silently entered the chamber. He was alone with the only person to ever turn down a seat on the Federation Council.

She was seated on a low divan, with a rug across her knees. Her hair was still black, except for two white streaks running through it, but her face was even more lined and withered than he remembered.

T'Pau saluted him formally, holding out one hand in the "V" signal of greeting. The spidery old fingers trembled a bit. *She's aged,* Spock thought, returning the greeting. "Live long and prosper, T'Pau."

"Why hast thou come in secrecy, and with no warning, Spock? Thy behavior is hardly courteous to thy parents." She spoke with a lisping inflection, voice barely above a whisper. She had not asked him to sit down, and that was a bad sign.

"I beg forgiveness, T'Pau. The reason for my visit is private—something I could discuss with you only. I seek your help, and your silence." His voice was level. Sharp obsidian eyes that belied the wizened face scrutinized him, and abruptly she nodded and gestured him to a seat. Spock sat down cross-legged on the hassock.

"I will hold thy silence. Speak."

"Several years ago, I went with my Captain and McCoy, whom you know, on a mission to warn the people of Sarpeidon that their planet's sun was about to nova. We discovered that all of the inhabitants had taken refuge in the past. Through an accident, McCoy and I were transported back in time to the planet's ice age. We were freezing to death, when a young woman appeared and led us to shelter. Her name was Zarabeth, and she had been exiled alone to the past through the actions of an enemy. She was trapped there due to a special conditioning process.

"I was—affected by the time change. I reverted to what our ancestors were, 5,000 years ago. Barbaric— I ate meat. And I sired a child on Zarabeth. I did not know it until a few days ago."

He'd seen revulsion in her eyes as he confessed to

27

eating meat, then she was impassive once more. She remained silent for a long moment, then stirred.

"Thy behavior was certainly no credit to thy family. But it is illogical to dwell on the sins of the past. Why has thou come to me?"

"I cannot leave my child to die alone on a planet never meant for our kind. I must bring him home, to the family. I will bring Zarabeth back, too, if I can reverse her conditioning. I owe her a chance to live. I request that you contact the Federation Council and arrange for me to use the Guardian of Forever. It's a time portal that can send me back there, to Sarpeidon's past. I have to try."

T'Pau considered for a long moment, eyes hooded. "Yes. Thee must try. This child will be thy heir if thee dies without further issue. And thee has not entered kunat kalifee with another. We must protect the succession."

Spock realized he had been holding his breath, and let it out slowly. The worst was over.

"I've prepared a report stating all the information you will need to contact the Council, T'Pau. It gives the specifics of the case, and the code signs to identify the time portal. It names the search-party members, and the possible number of persons transported from the past. If your request is denied, send a subspace message to Captain Kirk on the *Enterprise.*"

She took the document and looked at him. "I will contact the Council immediately. Do thou be careful. What will thee do when thee finds them?"

Spock paused, at a loss. He hadn't thought beyond the bare fact of the child's existence, and his duty. "I'll bring them back to the present, and . . ." he hesitated again.

Her glance was sharp. "I take it that means thee hast not thought that far ahead? Remember, Spock. This son of yours is a person. Each being has its own dignity and life. Allow thy son this dignity. He is thy issue—but not thee. Remember our symbol," she touched the IDIC medal hanging on her shrunken

28

chest. "Treasure the differences, as well as the similarities."

Spock didn't understand her words, except intellectually. He nodded absently, preoccupied with the logistics of getting himself out of the house and to the spaceport without being recognized. At T'Pau's signal, he rose, saluted her. "I thank you, T'Pau. Have I your leave?"

She nodded, looking suddenly weary. "Thee hast leave to go, Spock. I will have Sandar take thee to the spaceport. I will not inform thy parents of thy visit, but remember this: if thee is successful, they will know, and so will all our people. *Thee* must accept what thou has done; for thy good, and for the good of thy child. Live long and prosper, Spock." She returned his salute, and beckoned to Sandar, her aide, who had appeared as if by magic.

Spock bowed slightly. "Peace and long life, T'Pau." In silence, he left the chamber.

Chapter III

Kirk sat in the section of the rec deck that had temporarily been converted into a theater, watching *H.M.S. Pinafore,* but his attention wasn't on the stage. Tonight his ship had docked at Star Base 11, and Spock was overdue. Tomorrow morning at 0900, the Star Fleet technicians would swarm aboard for her two-week inspection and repair detail. If Spock and he didn't get started within twenty-four hours, they couldn't make it halfway across the sector to the Guardian and back within the allotted time, and the scheduled date to report for duty might find the *Enterprise* without her First Officer and her Captain.

Of course, it was entirely possible that she would be without them even if they left this minute. During Spock's absence, Kirk had studied the cave paintings and all the available data on Sarpeidon's ice age. It seemed likely that if somehow the climate missed killing you, the wildlife would cheerfully oblige. The chances of *anyone* surviving in that environment seemed remote—especially a child.

Kirk had considered trying to talk Spock out of this crazy venture, but abandoned the idea when he recalled the look in the Vulcan's eyes. And he couldn't let him go alone.

The audience around him was standing and applauding enthusiastically. The Captain hastily joined them and watched Scotty dash backstage and drag a reluctant Uhura out to take a bow. The crew roared when the Chief Engineer gave the Chief Communications Officer a resounding kiss. As Kirk stood among his cheering crew, he saw the person he'd been waiting for enter the rec deck through one of the side entrances and stand searching the faces.

Spock stood braced against the bulkhead as Kirk joined him, as though his body might fall without the support. The normally impeccably-groomed fringe of dark bangs was rumpled, and the face beneath looked more exhausted than the last time Kirk had seen the Vulcan.

"You look terrible! What the hell have you been—" Kirk began, then interrupted himself. "We've *got* to hurry, or we'll miss that supply shuttle. I've got our gear in my quarters. All set on your end?"

In Kirk's quarters, both officers changed into durable scouting coveralls, and packed their camping and cold-weather gear into kits. "I raided sickbay when McCoy was out last week, and got a medical kit together." Kirk said. "Should we bring phasers? Mine didn't work last time we were on Sarpeidon."

"I investigated that, and found that the atavachron—their time portal—was set to automatically negate the effectiveness of any weapon that passed through it. A precautionary measure to prevent someone from the future from ruling a past society. Our phasers will work this time."

"Good. I'd hate to depend on rocks and fists against some of the life-forms I read about. You ready?"

"Ready, Captain."

The two officers headed for the turbo-lift, carrying their kits. Kirk glanced at the Vulcan. "What kept you? I was beginning to think you weren't going to make it back."

"I was forced to return aboard a robot freighter. There were no faster ships available."

Kirk looked sympathetic. "No wonder you look bad. Tried that myself once, when I was in the Academy. Went to visit a . . . friend. By the time I arrived, she wouldn't have anything to do with me. Not that I blame her. Well, at least our transport to the Guardian won't be that bad. We're traveling aboard the supply ship. You can clean up when we board her. Until then, I'll try and look as if I'm not with you." They reached the turbo-lift. "Transporter," the Captain said, and the doors snapped shut.

And promptly whooshed back open again. A red light began flashing on the lift's instrument panel.

"Who the hell pushed the override?" Kirk thumbed buttons. Reluctantly, the doors began closing. From the corridor they heard a staccato pound of running footsteps, then a booted leg was thrust through the panels, which snapped open again. McCoy, dressed in scouting coveralls and toting a kit, dived in.

"Whew," he slumped against the wall as the turbo-lift started off, "I thought I was going to miss you two!"

The Captain stared, then as the meaning of the Doctor's clothing and equipment dawned, his eyes hardened. "No, you don't, Bones—" he began.

Spock was saying, "Doctor McCoy, your presence is highly—"

"Shut up, both of you!" McCoy snapped. Spock's eyebrow continued its climb as the Medical Officer growled, "Stow the arguments. You didn't really think I was going to let you go tearing off on the crazy quest without me, did you? Uh-uh." He shook his head. "After all, I've had more experience at being frostbitten than either of you. And beautiful, balmy Sarpeidon is just the right place to spend my leave." He grinned, then sobered. "Besides, what if one of you gets hurt—or you need medical help for the kid?"

Kirk stared. "How do you know about that?"

McCoy jerked his head at Spock. "I was with him, remember? And I saw the paintings. You don't have to be a Vulcan to add up one plus one equals three. Give me a little credit, Jim."

"Bones." Kirk's tone was ominous. "You're getting off this lift, and back to sickbay. That's an order."

"You forget, Captain. I'm on leave, just like you two. You can't tell me where to spend it. Besides, I've got an ace in the hole. I've been going over the medical information from Sarpeidon's Library for the last couple of weeks, and I've figured out a way to medically reverse Zarabeth's conditioning. If you want the process, then I go with it."

Kirk scowled. "Blackmail, Doctor."

"A common means of persuasion aboard this vessel, Captain." Spock commented. Kirk gave him a quick look, but the Vulcan was staring straight ahead, expressionless.

"What did you pack in your kit?" the Captain asked, after a pause.

McCoy smiled triumphantly. "The same stuff you did. I asked the computer for a list of everything you requisitioned from supply for the last week."

"Logical," murmured Spock. The lift stopped.

Kirk snapped his fingers. "Bones, you can't go along, no matter if we want to take you or not. T'Pau only requested clearance for two, didn't she?" He regarded the Vulcan hopefully.

"I specified clearance for three, Captain. Taking into account Doctor McCoy's predictable penchant for rushing in where angels fear to tread, I reasoned he would attempt this. There is usually a logical pattern to his illogical behavior."

They were standing on the transporter pads listening to the whine of the 20-second delay before McCoy thought of a suitably scathing reply. He opened his mouth to deliver it, but the transporter beams caught them, and they dissolved into triple pillars of shimmer.

Chapter IV

The planet hasn't changed, Kirk thought, as he looked around. The same silvery sky, shading to black overhead, pockmarked with stars. The same ruins, columns fallen and tumbled, some nearly intact, others barely discernible from the natural rocks. The same cold wind, whining like a lost spirit. The same aura of terrible age. The memories, crowding his mind, of the last time. He'd thought it forgotten, buried, but being here, standing in this desolation, brought back the agony. *Edith . . .* his mind whispered.

"I didn't notice much of the landscape last time," McCoy said, as he and Spock stood apart. "Spooky. That wind gets to you after a while. . . . Look, there's what looks like the shell of a temple or something over there." He pointed. The Vulcan stopped fiddling with his tricorder and looked up.

"The Guardian of Forever lies in that direction, Doctor. For some reason, the ruins are most intact, closer to the time portal." Spock looked back at his tricorder.

"Guardian of Forever . . . sounds like the name of a damn mortuary. . . ." the Doctor mumbled. Spock ignored him. McCoy looked at his companion and shook his head. The Vulcan had been too quiet on the three-day voyage. He hadn't joined the two-day poker game that had left McCoy considerably richer, which was no surprise, but he hadn't joined the conversation either. The Doctor was worried about him.

"Hey!" The cheerful hail came from behind them. They turned to see a small, stocky, gray-haired woman approaching. Behind her, and about 150 meters away was a small pre-fab building, whose sides matched the grayness around them so closely that it had escaped their notice.

The woman reached them, puffing a little, and pointed a finger at each of them in turn. "Kirk, Spock, McCoy. I'm Vargas. How do you do?"

"Fine, thank you," Kirk said, smiling.

"Been expecting you. Let's get this stuff back home, and we can talk over a cup of coffee. Real coffee, too." She distributed anti-grav units, and they headed for the building, piloting the supplies and their kits.

The interior of the archeologists' camp was a pleasant contrast to its drab outside. The walls were covered with paintings and posters, and there were comfortable rugs underfoot. The building housed several labs, a large sitting room, bedrooms for the nine staff members, a kitchen large enough for all of them to eat in and a small but well-stocked library. Doctor Vargas proudly showed them around, introducing them to the eight members of her staff.

After the formalities were completed, the four of them gathered in the kitchen for the promised coffee. Vargas stirred hers emphatically, then fixed her visitors with a narrow-eyed glare. "Please explain to me how the *hell* you managed to get permission to use the Guardian. Who do you know?"

"Doctor Vargas, we are on a rescue mission." Spock looked grave. "As you already know, the planet we've been given permission to visit was destroyed two years ago. Our mission can have no effect on its history, especially since the persons we intend to rescue are in an isolated area, out of their proper time stream. Due to an accident, a . . . member of my family was marooned back in the planet's last ice age, with a native of Sarpeidon who was exiled to the past. We intend to bring both of them to the present."

McCoy heard the lie, and choked on his coffee. Kirk kicked him sharply under the table. The byplay went unnoticed, as Vargas replied, "I must abide by my orders, but I think this is a big mistake. The persons stationed here are all top-ranked archeologists and historians, yet even we are not permitted to go back in time. We are only allowed to observe and record the history pictures, sift the ruins and try to understand the race that lived here when life on Earth was confined to one-celled creatures in the sea. It's too dangerous to allow travel though the time portal—as you three already know!"

"We know." Spock toyed with his spoon, and didn't meet her eyes. "We shall take all precautions to avoid any contact with the indigenous life. Fortunately, the developing humanoid race—which at the time of our visit was just beginning a cultural and technological advance that changed them from nomadic primitives to a city-state with an agrarian economy—this developing race occupied the southern hemisphere of the planet only. We will be searching approximately eight thousand kilometers north of the equator."

Vargas sighed. "I know that you'll be careful, but you can't convince me that anything is worth the risk involved. If only one small event in history happens or doesn't happen . . ."

Or one person dies or doesn't die . . . Kirk supplemented mentally. He nodded, and said, "We fully understand the danger, Doctor Vargas. Have you headed this expedition ever since the *Enterprise* discovered the Guardian?"

"Yes. It's been four years now. We are a quasi-permanent expedition here. The Federation cannot take any chances of a security leak, for obvious reasons. Anyone wishing to leave must undergo memory suppression and hypno-conditioning."

"Frankly, I'm surprised more protection isn't apparent, ma'am." McCoy observed, glancing around as though he half-expected armed guards stationed in the kitchen.

Vargas chuckled, her blue eyes following the Medical Officer's gaze. "No, Doctor McCoy, you won't find artillery or explosives in the cupboards! Still, we're protected here. A Federation starship is assigned a monthly tour of duty to patrol this system. This month it's the *Exeter*. Next month it will be the *Potemkin*. Of course they don't know what it is they're protecting—they think they're nursemaiding a valuable archeological discovery—which is the truth, after all. But I'll wager you're the only starship Captain in the fleet that knows the real properties of the Guardian, Captain Kirk. So, I think we're safe here."

"Let's hope so." Kirk finished the contents of his cup. "Thank you for the coffee. I'd forgotten how good the real stuff tastes."

"They give us the best here. When are you going to attempt the time portal?"

"Immediately." Spock's voice was abrupt, and he got up from the table and left the room.

Vargas looked startled, and Kirk said, "He's impatient to get started. He didn't tell you that this relative of his is a child—we can only hope that he's still alive."

Vargas' gaze softened. "I understand better, now. I have a daughter, Anna. I talk to her on the subspace radio sometimes. . . ."

She led the way to the Guardian. It stood amid the ruins, resembling nothing so much as a large, irregularly hewn stone doughnut. The primitive shaping gave no hint of the strange power it possessed.

As they approached, it was dull gray, the color of the ruins, and its central hole was clear, allowing them to see the ruined shape of the temple McCoy had pointed out earlier.

Spock was there ahead of them, their kits at his feet, tricorder in hand. The Vulcan had spent weeks here, shortly after the Guardian's discovery, along with two other scientists—top minds in the Federation—studying the time portal. At the end of their stay, they were still at a loss to say how the Guardian worked; how it channeled its energy into time currents, or where that energy came from. They were unable even to agree on whether the entity was a computer of incredible complexity, or whether it was a life-form. As he stood before it now, Kirk thought privately that man simply wasn't capable of comprehending the nature of the Guardian—yet.

But man could make use of what he did not understand. Spock walked forward, tricorder ready. "Greetings." The Vulcan's voice, usually so matter-of-fact, held awe, and he saluted the stone shape in the manner of his people. "I am Spock, and have traveled with you once before. Can you show me the history of the planet Sarpeidon, that formerly circled the star Beta Niobe?"

It always took a question to evoke a response from the Guardian, and now the stone shape flickered, lighting translucently from within. A deep, strangely warm voice rang out. "I can show you Sarpeidon's past. It has no future. Behold."

The middle of the time portal was filled with vapor, then swirling images, too fast for the eye to catch and remember. Suggestions of volcanoes, mammoth reptile-like animals, mud villages, stone cities, seas, boats, armies, steel and glass cities, and finally, a blinding light that made all of them shield their eyes. During the entire presentation, which lasted perhaps a minute and a half, Spock's tricorder whirred at double-speed.

The central viewport was clear again, and Kirk joined the First Officer who was bent over the tricorder. "Get it all, Spock?"

"Yes." The Vulcan's voice was hollow. "I believe I've managed to isolate the correct period during the planet's last ice age. The neutron dating system used on the paintings is, fortunately, quite accurate. Our problem is not *when* to jump, but *where* we shall nd up on Sarpeidon's surface. We cannot search the ntire planet."

"I hadn't thought of that." Kirk glanced at the ow-quiescent Guardian. "That's a real problem."

"I have in mind a possible solution. The power of ne time portal is vast. The Guardian can probably et us down in the correct location—if I can com- nunicate our desire to it. I shall attempt it." The Vulcan made a final adjustment to his tricorder, and urned back to face the rough-hewn form. His voice vas low, tense.

"Guardian. Can you differentiate between one life- orm and another? For instance, can you discern that am of a different species than my companions?"

"You are of a different species within yourself." 'he Guardian intoned. Spock, accustomed to the en- ity's circumlocutions, nodded, apparently satisfied hat the answer was an affirmative one.

"Very well. There is a life-form located in Sar- •eidon's last ice age that is of the same species as . We are of one blood and kin. I wish to locate this ife-form. Is it possible for us to be delivered to this ocation when we go through the portal?"

Short silence. Then the voice boomed out again, eemingly from the air around them. "All things are •ossible."

Spock's face, in the light reflected from the Guard- an, looked drawn, fleshless. The Vulcan persisted, ands clenched into fists, "Does that mean you will •e able to place us in the same location as this life- orm when we jump into time?"

The silence dragged on, broken only by the dron- ng of that desolate wind. Spock stood rigidly mo- ionless, seemingly willing an answer from the air around him. On impulse, McCoy stepped over to im, laid a hand on the First Officer's arm. The Doctor's voice was gentle. "Take it easy, Spock. Something tells me it'll be all right." The Vulcan glanced at him, no recognition in his eyes. Freeing his arm from the Doctor's grasp, he walked over to their supplies. Opening his kit, he began pulling on his therm-suit, a one-piece garment with attached face shield.

The Captain walked over and joined McCoy. "There's the answer, Bones. He's going, no matter what. Let's get ready."

When they were prepared for the jump, Spock made final adjustments to his tricorder, then spoke again to the time entity. "Guardian. Please show us Sarpeidon's past again, so we can locate and rescue the life-form that is similar to me."

Even the wind seemed to quiet for a moment as the scenario began to flicker in front of their eyes again. They stood, muscles twitching in anticipation, poised. From behind them somewhere came Vargas' voice. "Good luck—I envy you!"

"Be ready. Soon." Spock's eyes never left the tricorder. "One, two, three—now!" They all took a giant step, straight into the whirling vortex.

A star-flecked blackness, massive disorientation, giddiness. They staggered forward, blinking, then the cold air hit them, making their eyes water in the vicious wind. The entire world seemed to be white, gray and black, but the wind made it hard to tell. McCoy dug at his eyes, breath puffing in a steaming gasp, and swore.

"We *would* land at night." Kirk growled, fumbling for his face shield. "Put your mask up, Bones. You all right Spock?"

"Perfectly, Captain. I suggest we not attempt to move around in this wind. We seem to be on a level spot here, and fairly sheltered. There's a cliff to our right . . . if we can reach the lee of that . . ." The three stumbled a few meters to the right, and the wind died slightly. Fumbling, they set up the small therm-tent they'd brought.

Inside the comparative warmth and light of the tent, they relaxed, looking at each other. McCoy's sense of humor reasserted itself as he observed his friends,

They looked like large insects, he thought, with their faceted eye coverings and shiny scaled insulators covering their mouths and noses. "Looks like Halloween in here," the Doctor chuckled, pulling his face shield off. He wagged a finger accusingly at the Vulcan as the First Officer brushed snow out of his hair. "I'll tell you something, Spock. You sure have a talent for picking nice places to spend our first leave in way over a year." McCoy shook his head at Kirk, who was grinning, and continued, "Beautiful warm sunlight, gorgeous countryside. The women are welcoming, the natives are friend—" The Medical Officer broke off abruptly as something roared outside. Something very large, by the sound of it.

They sat in silence, as the roar came again, dying away into a bubbling wail, and then there was only the sound of the wind, and the swish of the snow against the tent. McCoy swallowed.

"What was that?" he asked, very quietly.

"Probably a sithar, Bones." Kirk supplied, helpfully. "Very large predator. Looks like a cross between a musk ox and a lion. You remember, there was one painted on the wall. Scientists estimated them to be about the size of an Earth buffalo."

"Carnivorous?" McCoy asked, still in that quiet tone. Spock raised an eyebrow and glanced at Kirk, whose smile broadened.

"Sure." Kirk replied. "Their favorite meal is Chief Surgeons who don't have the sense to listen to their Commanding Officers."

McCoy glared at him, then grinned sheepishly. "Guess I did kind of crash the party. But, dammit, you may need me!" He paused, then said, "Well, what'll we do for the rest of the night? Sit around and listen to that thing howl for its supper? Or—" he dug in his suit's pockets, "we could have a friendly little game. I brought my cards . . ."

Kirk shoved him with his boot. "I'd rather be eaten by a sithar than lose my shirt to you again. I'm turning in."

The Doctor turned to the Vulcan. "What about it, Spock? Deuces wild?"

His mouth quirked a bit at the corners, as the First Officer shook his head. "I, too, am fatigued, Doctor. Perhaps the sithar will join you for a game—if you ask it politely."

McCoy lay in the dark, listening to the wind over Kirk's snores. It was a long time before he slept.

Chapter V

Kirk awakened in the morning to find Spock gone. He hastily pulled on his therm-suit and left the Doctor sleeping peacefully. As he opened the flap of the tent, he saw his First Officer standing a few meters away, and joined him as he stood surveying the landscape.

The storm had gone, and the air was cold and clear. Beta Niobe was rising, swollen and blood-colored, in a pale lavender sky that shaded to deep purple the undersides of the remaining storm clouds. They'd camped in a sheltered hollow at the base of a jagged cliff that rose on the right until it blocked the sky. Before them was a large, U-shaped valley, flanked by the cliffs. Snow lay in patches on top of short, mossy ground cover, pale aqua in color. The valley was dotted with many small, narrow lakes, the wind riffling their sapphire water. Far in the distance, at the end of his vision, Kirk could make out a herd of animals. He was aware that McCoy had joined him, and turned around at the sound of the Doctor's startled gasp.

Behind and to their left, a frozen tidal wave loomed. From where Kirk stood it might have been a quarter of a kilometer away, a wall of turquoise ice studded with boulders. The glacier was at least three hundred meters high, and Kirk craned his neck trying to see where it ended.

"Damn," McCoy commented, inadequately. "You ever see one of these things before, Jim?"

"I've skied on them, in Colorado, but I never saw

one this big in the Rockies. I wonder how big it is, how far it goes?"

Spock looked up from his tricorder. "The glacier is only a part of a larger ice sheet that extends northward as far as my tricorder range."

"I guess the wind blows down off the ice sheet—how cold is it?" Kirk slipped his hand out of his glove, tested the air.

"The present temperature is −10° Celsius, but the wind chill makes it feel colder than that. The temperature during the middle of the day will probably rise to above freezing," Spock replied.

"Actually, it's not as cold as I thought an ice age would be," McCoy commented. "Nothing like the last time we were here."

"We are fortunate that we've arrived during the late spring, instead of winter this time, Doctor," Spock said.

"This is spring?" McCoy was taken aback.

"I think Dante wrote about this place," mused Kirk. "Just knowing that damned sun is going to blow gives me the shivers. See the typical pattern of the corona? Looks like it could go any minute."

"We know that Beta Niobe will not nova for 5,000 years, Captain. It is illogical to waste time speculating on impossibilities. I suggest we begin searching, keeping in touch by communicator." Spock betrayed impatience, as he scanned the area again with his tricorder.

"Any life-form readings, Spock?" McCoy wanted to know.

"Several, Doctor, but I believe they belong to some of the higher animals. However, my reception is limited by the mountain ranges."

"We must be pretty far above sea level," Kirk said. "The air feels thin."

"You are correct, Captain. We are approximately 2000 meters above sea level, and this atmosphere is thinner than Earth normal. The gravity is 1.43 times that of Earth's. You and Doctor McCoy should be careful until you become acclimated."

"Got any tri-ox in your kit, Bones?" Kirk asked.

McCoy smiled. "You mean you trust me to give you another shot of that stuff?"

Spock stirred impatiently. "I suggest we set out. Remember to keep your face shields on."

"Why? Doesn't seem that cold, except for the wind." Kirk said.

The Vulcan gestured with the tricorder. "My readings indicate that this area, typical of the tundra ecology, is teeming with insect life, similar to Earth mosquitoes. Let's keep to the edge of the valley—remember that the cave was located along a ridge of some kind. It could be set in one of these cliffs. Also look for mineral deposits that could indicate the presence of hot springs. The cave was heated by one."

"Spock, don't you remember anything about the area from when you were here before? Landmarks? We could take weeks, just searching to decide if the Guardian put us down in the right place, or time." Kirk surveyed the rough terrain, dismayed.

"Captain, we were in the middle of a blizzard, without protective clothing or face shields. Doctor McCoy was freezing to death, and I was attempting to carry him. It was impossible to memorize landmarks." Spock was more than a bit exasperated.

"I guess that is asking a lot. We can only hope that the Guardian didn't make à mistake. Bones, you go left, Spock, you can go right, and I'll stay in the middle. Let's keep in sight if possible. Let's go."

By the time Beta Niobe splashed the patches of snow crimson, the three men met back at their starting place. Kirk and McCoy, too tired to talk, gulped rations and crawled into their sleeping bags before the stars appeared. Spock, more accustomed to the higher gravity, sat outside the tent alone, until the cold drove him inside. None of them had seen anything that even hinted at intelligent life—only the desolate sameness of the tundra.

Two days passed, and the pattern of the first day was repeated. Search the valley and along the face of the glacier, meet back at a prearranged point for food, then, exhausted, sleep. Spock was the only one not affected by the altitude or the physical demands of the search. The mental strain was another thing. The First Officer looked drawn and haggard, and McCoy suspected he wasn't sleeping much, a guess confirmed their third night on Sarpeidon.

The Doctor roused groggily at the echo of a distant combat, and heard the Vulcan dictating to his tricorder in a low voice. ". . . soil samples indicate that the permafrost layer is extensive, and the tundra-like ground covering shows the typical 'patterned ground' hexagonal configuration. Geologically—" McCoy raised himself on an elbow.

"Spock, what the hell are you doing? What time is it?"

"It is zero-one-thirty-five point zero-two, local time, Doctor McCoy."

"Why aren't you asleep?"

"As you know, Vulcans can go without sleep for extended periods of time. I'm making notes on my tricorder scannings for a research paper, to be entitled, 'Geological and Ecological Conditions—'

"Spock, what the *hell* are you doing?" Kirk interrupted.

"I regret that I disturbed you, Captain. I was dictating notes for a research paper."

"Can't you sleep?" Kirk sounded concerned. "Bones can give you something."

McCoy reached for his medical kit in the dark, but Spock's voice stopped him. "Unnecessary, Doctor. I can induce sleep if necessary—I won't require one of your potions."

The Medical Officer's voice was peevish. "Well induce it then, and let us all get some rest." He

46

reached up and turned on the light, surveyed the First Officer critically. "Look at you—Vulcans don't need sleep, my ass. You're ready to drop." His expression changed to one of concern. "You're not helping that kid out there by staying awake worrying about him."

Nobody had referred to the object of their search since they'd left the *Enterprise,* and Spock obviously found the Doctor's bluntness painful. "It is easy for you to reach that conclusion, Doctor, since the reason for this mission is not your responsibility, it is mine. While recrimination is not logical, it is—"

"Unnecessary." Kirk cut in. "Your situation is hardly unique, Mr. Spock. After all, the same kind of thing has been happening to men and women ever since we began visiting other planets. Even I have—" The Captain broke off as his two officers exchanged a sidelong glance. "What's that supposed to mean?" he demanded.

"Nothing, Jim," McCoy said, with studied innocence. "Nothing at all. I think we should get some more rest."

It was the following afternoon when McCoy found the hot spring. He let out a yelp over his communicator that brought the others running. They found the Doctor sitting on his heels, looking at a depression in the rocks. Steam rose out of it, and the rock itself was encrusted with mineral deposits in bright reds, blues, greens and yellows. Spock scanned the area again, but reported no life-forms within range. They set out to follow the path of the underground river, as it wound along the base of the cliffs.

The excitement of locating the hot spring held them until sunset, when they made camp, but was gradually replaced by depression. Each of them knew that if they didn't locate any concrete signs of life within the next two days, they would be forced to go back and try the Guardian again. After their meal, Kirk and McCoy played double solitaire for a while, but the game soon languished. Finally they all just sat, listening to the wind.

McCoy shivered. "Did you hook up the distort tonight, Spock?"

"Yes, Doctor. I have done so every night. Why?"

"Nothing—I have this feeling something's watching us. This place gets on your nerves." The Doctor abruptly cut, then shuffled the deck of cards with a snap that made them all jump.

Kirk nodded. "I know what you mean, Bones. I've been feeling the same way. Too much imagination—that wind's enough to shake anybody. You're lucky Vulcans are immune to it, Spock."

The First Officer looked thoughtful. "Perhaps it is a result of fatigue, Captain, because the same impression has been in my mind—that something is watching us. It started several hours ago. . . ."

Startled, Kirk and McCoy nodded corroboration. Spock raised an eyebrow. "Since all of us share the same impression, starting at about the same time, it is possible that we *are* under observation. A predator may be stalking us."

"You're probably right, Spock," the Captain said. "We've been lucky we haven't encountered any animal life before now. Tomorrow we'll stay together. Make sure your phasers are fully charged."

The next morning dawned as bright and clear as the three previous ones. "We've been lucky with the weather, anyway," Kirk commented, as they picked their way along the rocky streambed, an icy counterpart to the boiling river that flowed beneath the cliff.

"We've been lucky with just about everything except finding the object of our search, Jim." McCoy raised a sardonic eyebrow. "I'll trade the good weather and the lack of predators for one sight of . . ." Spock had stopped so suddenly that the Doctor bumped into him.

"I'm picking up something on my tricorder." The

Vulcan's tone of voice, usually so matter-of-fact, betrayed excitement.

McCoy narrowed his eyes, scanning the ridge ahead of him. With a wordless exclamation, he pushed Spock out of his way and moved unerringly to a portion of the rocky wall. Running his hands over its ice-rimed surface, he turned his head to address the others. "I think this is where we came through the atavachron!"

The Vulcan was beside him in a few running steps. "You are correct, Doctor. That means that the cave is—" Spock broke off, conscious of an irrational dread. *He did not want to look for the cave.* Confused, he shook his head, feelings flooding his mind . . . *fear . . . hate . . . anger.* . . . He gasped, swayed, put both his hands to his head, no longer aware of his companions, feeling only those alien emotions. Alien! They came from outside his own mind . . . an invasion. As his knees began to buckle from the assault, he marshalled himself and began to fight back.

Power! It was strong, but . . . *the mind rules . . . my mind rules.* . . . *Mine!* The link snapped, and he was free, to find Kirk and McCoy holding his arms. Slowly his vision cleared, and he saw a dark opening in the rocks some distance away that he recognized. As he stared, a figure darted from behind a boulder and ran for the cave.

Somehow he had shaken off Kirk and McCoy, and was running himself, faster than he'd ever moved in his life. He could hear the others as they came pelting after him. Spock had nearly reached the cave opening when a rock caught him in the shoulder. He staggered, nearly fell, then Kirk and McCoy were beside him and they were all staring at the being that crouched, back against the cliff wall.

It was humanoid, but so swathed in furs that it was impossible to tell more. Spock stepped forward, and a snarl came from the recesses of the hood. The sound was not human.

It's Zarabeth, thought McCoy. *Too tall for a chila She's gone mad with the loneliness*. As he steppe in front of the Vulcan, opening his mouth to spea reassuringly, the ragged figure moved with the spee of desperation, and a good-sized rock caught th Doctor in the midsection. McCoy gasped and fell Kirk leaped forward, saw the flash of a knife, lashe out with his foot, and heard the weapon ring agains the wall. Hands fastened themselves around hi throat. The Captain flung himself backward, one kne coming up viciously, felt his assailant twist to avoi the blow, and the steely fingers loosened. He du; his thumbs into the pressure points in the wrists, an when they slipped, rolled free, air scorching hi throat. He struck out, trying to push away com pletely, felt teeth sink into his wrist, and then th creature sagged half on top of him, limp.

Spock released his hand from the junction of necl and shoulder, as the Captain scrambled up, rubbin; his throat. "Bones all right?" he croaked, and sav McCoy staggering toward them, medical tricorde ready. They stood back as the Doctor ran his scanne over the mound of skins, then looked up. "Humanoi . . . Vulcan . . . and something else. Help me turi him over."

The concealing hood fell back, to reveal the face bearded, with long dark hair tied back. The face or the cave wall, but older, that of a man in his mid twenties. McCoy sat back on his heels, staring "Looks like we miscalculated a bit. . . . But bette late than never, I suppose." He looked up at Spock then back again at his unconscious patient. "The ra cial characteristics are unmistakable, aren't they?"

Chapter VI

Kirk couldn't see Spock's face, but the Vulcan sounded dazed, hesitant. "Perhaps we'd better move . . . him . . . into the cave. It will be warm here. . . ."

The Captain waited for a second, but the other didn't move, so he nodded to McCoy and the two of them carried the limp form into the cave. Kirk recognized the interior from the pictures, but his attention was mostly for Spock, who followed at a distance. As soon as they laid their burden on a pile of furs, he left the Doctor and turned back to his First Officer.

He'd removed his face shield, but his features were still a mask, skin stretched tight over bone, eyes blank, hooded. *He's in shock,* Kirk thought, deeply concerned, *and that's not so surprising. To find an adult when we expected a child . . . even to find anyone at all. . . . How would I feel—react? Probably the same. . . .* Hesitantly, he put a hand on his friend's arm. Spock did not acknowledge the gesture outwardly, but there was an easing of tension in the muscles beneath Kirk's fingers.

The Captain removed his face shield, pushed back his hood, then returned to McCoy and his patient. Beneath the furs, the young man wore a leather tunic, and McCoy had loosened the front lacings and bared the chest. Beneath a surface layer of dirt and black hair, bones and ribs showed clearly. The Doctor pressed several injections into his patient's shoulder, and looked up at Kirk. "He should be coming around

in a minute. He's in remarkably good shape fo
someone who must've been living on the edge o
starvation for years. It's incredible he managed t
survive at all. I wonder where Zarabeth is?"

"I don't see another sleeping place," Kirk said
glancing around. "Have you given him something t
calm him down?" The Captain rubbed his bruise
neck as McCoy swabbed the blood off his wrist. "
don't care to take a chance on subduing him again."
He glanced across the cave at Spock, who was sti
turned away, and lowered his voice. "He's inherite
some of his father's strength along with those ears."

"I don't think he'll struggle when he sees ou
faces." McCoy said, thoughtfully running his med
ical scanner. "I think he was frightened by our fac
shields—God knows that if you didn't know wha
they were, you'd think they were our real features.
He turned his head, addressed the Vulcan. "H
should've come around by now, Spock. Did you d
anything to account for this prolonged unconscious
ness?"

The First Officer shook his head as he approached
He stood over them, not too near, looking down a
the younger man.

"Of course, the struggle may have affected him—
he's malnourished. Jim walloped him good a coupl
of times, too. . . ." McCoy glanced at the Vulcan'
stony lack of expression, and continued under hi
breath, "Actually, you should be grateful he's alive
and old enough to take care of himself. . . . If
remember, you don't relate very well to infants." H
ran the scanner again, then nodded. "He's comin
around now."

The leather-clad figure stirred and moaned. Th
eyes opened. Gray, wide with fear, then calming a
they slowly took in McCoy's friendly blue eyes an
dark hair, Kirk's regular features and smile. The
traveled upward, glanced at Spock, whose feature
were shadowed by the hood of his therm-suit, an
returned to the two in front of him. The young ma

at up a bit unsteadily, rubbing his neck. The eyes were wide now with questions.

The Captain glanced at his First Officer, still silent and removed, then wryly assumed his best visiting-diplomat manner. "Sorry we didn't get off to a better start. We should've remembered how our face masks would look to someone who hadn't seen before. You must be Zarabeth's son."

The younger man nodded, obviously startled, then said haltingly, in the tones of one who has talked only to himself for a long time. "Yes . . . I am Zarabeth's son. I'm Zar." Then gathering speed, "Who are you? Were you looking for me? Where did you come from?" His voice was pleasant, not as deep as Spock's, his speech precise.

"I'm Captain Kirk of the Starship *Enterprise*. My Chief Medical Officer, Doctor Leonard McCoy." The Captain gestured at the Doctor, who smiled. The gray eyes moved across the cave, fixed on the Vulcan, as Kirk hesitated. "And my First Officer, Mr. Spock."

Still watching Spock intently, Zar got slowly to his feet, as McCoy put a hand out to steady him. The Doctor's voice was gentle. "Where's Zarabeth?"

His gaze never left Spock as the young man answered absently, though not without pain, "She . . . dead. Killed when she fell into a crevasse in the ice, seven summers past." Slowly, as though Kirk and McCoy were no longer present, he walked between them and halted in front of the Vulcan.

Their eyes were on a level as Zar said quietly, "Spock . . . First Officer of the *Enterprise* . . . my father." A flat statement, hanging in the stillness.

Spock drew a long breath. "Yes."

It was startling to see a grin spread over the younger man's expressionless features, a look of such genuine warmth and happiness that the Humans found themselves smiling too. Zar's clenched fists relaxed, and for a moment Kirk worried that he might throw his arms around the Vulcan, but something in that remote figure, hands clasped behind his back, seemed

53

to deter him. "I'm glad you've come, sir," he sai simply. It was the most sincere statement the Captai had ever heard. The incredible smile was still on th bearded countenance as he turned back to the Hu mans. "I am glad you're here, too. Did all of yo come here to find me?"

"Yes, we've been searching for four days, now. Kirk said.

"How did you get here? My mother told me man times about the two men who came from the futur but she said that the world was going to blow up the atavachron must've been destroyed, too."

"We used another method of finding you. A tim portal called the Guardian of Forever. You're rig about the destruction. In our present, this planet n longer exists." the Captain explained.

The younger man nodded as he pushed long ha out of his eyes and tightened the leather thong at th back of his neck. Pulling his tunic across his ches he began relacing it. "I followed you," he saic without looking up. "I didn't know who you wer I didn't even suspect. I thought you were aliens fror another time, or another world. . . . I didn't eve realize you were *people*. Then you trapped me whe I tried to make you go away."

McCoy grinned ruefully. "That was a mistake, a right. You sure can fight, son. Were you watchin us long?"

"Since last night. I was over-mountain, hunting and I saw you just when it was dark. I tried to attac your camp last night, but there was a pain in m head, and I couldn't approach."

"The sonic distort," Kirk told him. "So that ex plains why we all kept thinking we were bein watched! I was afraid this planet of yours was a fecting our minds."

Zar nodded thoughtfully, then remembered long forgotten niceties, "Are you thirsty? I can bring som water. Or, if you're hungry, I have meat salted i the next chamber. And there's the kill outside, fresh.

"Thanks, but we've got rations with us." Kirk sat down on the floor, opening his kit, and took out four packets. Zar sat down cross-legged, broke his packet open, and sniffed it cautiously. Apparently reassured, wolfed the wafer with dispatch. *A real paradox,* the Captain thought, watching him lick the crumbs out of the packet. *He speaks like the well-bred product of a modern family, but his appearance and actions are those of a primitive.* He dug another wafer out of his kit, offered it to the younger man, who was trying not to eye it wistfully. "We've got plenty, Zar. Go ahead."

When McCoy handed him the third wafer, Zar hesitated before taking it, searching his memory. "Thank you." The last concentrate went down slowly, but completely. The hunter licked his fingers clean, neatly and efficiently, and sighed contentedly. "That was good. Like the things my mother had to eat when I was small."

"How old are you?" McCoy asked.

"I have twenty-five summers. Very soon it will be twenty-six."

"Then you've been alone here since you were nineteen?" Kirk asked.

"Yes."

The Captain shook his head. "Seven years is a long time to be alone."

The gray eyes were steady. "I didn't think about it much. It doesn't make sense to waste thought and time on a situation that can't be changed."

McCoy blinked. "Sounds like someone else I know," he mumbled.

Kirk looked at the entrance to the cave, where the shadows were lengthening. "Getting late. We'll have to be leaving soon."

"How will you return? There is no Guardian here."

"We don't know exactly how it works," Kirk said, "but the Guardian seems to sense when a mission is accomplished. When all of us are ready, we'll take

55

a step, together, and—there we are. Back in our ow
time."

"I wish I could see your time. I've looked at th
stars many nights, and thought how I would like
see them—visit them." Zar glanced diffidently
Spock. "I think it's in my blood—this wanting."

Evidently it hasn't occurred to him that he'll
going back with us, thought McCoy, waiting for th
Vulcan to clear up the misunderstanding. Whe
Spock remained silent, the Doctor said, "When v
leave, son, you're going with us. That was our who
reason for coming here."

The gray eyes widened in surprise, then the smi
flashed again, and he turned to Spock. "You're tal
ing me with you? To the starship, and the wonde
my mother told me about?"

The First Officer nodded silently.

"And there's always plenty to eat?"

Momentarily startled, the Captain realized that foc
must indeed be one of the most important things
the world to one who struggled for every meal. H
hastened to reassure him. "Yes, there's always plen
to eat—too much, sometimes," with a rueful glan
at McCoy.

Still watching Spock, Zar sobered. "You can
here, searched for me, though you didn't kno
me. . . . I'm grateful . . . Father. . . ."

The Vulcan didn't move, but Kirk had the distin
impression that he'd winced. Spock looked away, h
expression remote. "I didn't return before because
was unaware you—existed. It was a matter of fami
duty and loyalty."

"How did you find out that I . . . had been born?

"I saw an archeologist's photo of your paintin
on the cave wall. There was no other logical expl
nation for the racial characteristics." Absently, th
Vulcan pushed back his hood.

The younger man studied Spock's features in th
dim light. After a long moment, he mused, "I'd loc
at myself in my mother's mirror, sometimes, but

was small. So when I had fifteen summers, I painted my face on the cave wall, along with my hunting pictures. And, after she died, I talked to the face on the wall, sometimes. Now it's like looking at the wall again . . . Father. . . ."

"I would prefer that you address me by my name." Spock said stiffly. "I find the appellation 'father' inappropriate when used by a stranger."

The gray eyes were momentarily confused, then all animation drained from Zar's features, until they mirrored the Vulcan's stony ones. "As you wish, sir." Scrambling to his feet, he caught up his fur cloak, and left the cave.

There was a bitten-off expletive and a glare from McCoy, then the Doctor followed the younger man. Kirk was embarrassed, realizing that any comment on his part would be construed as interference. "I'll hurry Bones up," he said finally, and headed for the cave's entrance.

The Captain found Zar kneeling beside the body of a large horned animal, that he'd evidently dragged over the ice with a leather harness. Kirk stood beside the Doctor, watching, as the younger man took a fine-honed knife and began to skin the gutted carcass efficiently.

"How'd you get this?" Kirk asked, noting the absence of weapons, except for the knife.

"With this." Zar jerked his head at three round stones bound together with twisted thongs. "My mother made them—she read the idea in a book we had."

"A bola—" Kirk picked up the weapon, hefted and swung it experimentally. "Must take practice to bring down game with something like this. Is this how you got all your meat?"

"No, sometimes I use snares, or traps with rocks and bait."

"Why not a bow and arrow?" McCoy wanted to know.

The hunter sat back on his heels and waved a gory

hand at the valley. "They require wood, and there aren't any trees within five days journey of here, which is the farthest I've explored." He returned to his task.

"We've got to leave, soon, and I'm afraid you're not going to be able to take that meat with you." Kirk said, glancing at McCoy.

Zar stopped, then stood up slowly. "I didn't think—you're right of course, Captain." He wiped the blade on the animal's flank, sheathed it methodically. "It seems wasteful to leave it, though."

Silently, the three began gathering up the camping gear that was strewn outside the cave.

Inside, Spock stood alone, looking at the paintings. The colors were brighter than in the photos. He was confused, and felt irritation—directed at himself. The entire situation was disquieting—highly implausible. He was too young to have offspring "25 summers" old. The Vulcan's gaze traveled around the rocky chamber, and he saw several haunches of meat hanging in the corner. His stomach tightened, and he told himself that his reaction was illogical. Of course Zar ate meat—Zarabeth's supplies must be exhausted by now.

His eyes fell on the bed-place, spread with furs. He had a sudden, vivid memory of her—her mouth beneath his . . . her skin, warm and smooth . . . the soft little cries she made as he—Spock shook his head violently, shutting out images of an incident he hadn't acknowledged since it happened.

But it did happen—it's illogical to deny it. The proof is right outside. Spock realized that the cave was stiflingly hot, and that he was sweating.

Voices broke into his thoughts, and he turned to see the others. "We're ready to go," Kirk said, then addressed Zar. "Anything you want to take with you?"

The young man's gaze traveled slowly around the cave. "Just my books and weapons. I'll get them."

He returned in a few minutes with a hide-wrapped

bundle. "Ready?" Kirk asked, when Zar glanced around again, then hesitated.

"What is it, son?" McCoy's voice was gentle, as he imagined what it must feel like to leave the only home you'd ever known for an uncertain future—with a pointy-eared calculator who called you "stranger."

"It's just that I don't like the thought of leaving her . . . alone."

Kirk's brow furrowed. "Her? You mean your mother? I thought you said she fell into an ice crevasse."

"Yes. I climbed down as soon as I could, but . . . all I could do was retrieve her . . . body. The ground is too hard to dig, and there's no wood for a fire . . . I placed her in a cave under the ice sheet."

Kirk thought for a second. "You'd cremate the body if you could?" he asked, finally.

The younger man didn't meet his eyes, but nodded slowly.

"Well, we have our phasers, we can do that. Where is she?"

"I'll show you."

There was a winding passage at the back of the cave. After the first few steps, the darkness was total, but their guide led them with the ease of one who'd traveled the way often. Kirk was conscious of McCoy behind him, nearly treading on his heels, and couldn't blame the Doctor. *To be lost in this labyrinth . . .* Far behind him, he could hear another set of footfalls echoing.

There was a faint blue-green glow ahead of him, and his light-starved eyes seized on it greedily. The light grew stronger, and finally they stepped out of the passage into an area lit faintly by that watery glow. Kirk heard McCoy's indrawn breath.

The cavern was large, with irregular rocky walls. In the center of the chamber, light filtered rosy from a glimpse of sky high overhead that was touched by Beta Niobe's setting rays. The rest of the cavern was shadowed by the thickness of the surrounding ice sheet, and the Captain could barely make out the thin glaze of ice that covered the walls and floor. The place was filled with a terrible, still cold. Kirk's eyes were drawn to a small raised platform in the center.

She lay on one large fur robe, covered by another. Her hands were clasped together on her breast, and her eyes were closed. In the soft light, the frozen features bore a flush that mimicked life.

"Just as I remember her." McCoy's voice came softly from beside him. Kirk shivered, caught in the spell cast by that still face.

"She looks as if she could be awakened, if only . . ." the Captain's whisper trailed off. There was a rustle behind him, and he knew that Spock stood there, in the mouth of the tunnel. He resisted the urge to turn and look at the Vulcan.

Zar moved foward, and hesitated beside the platform for a long moment, loose hair hiding his features as he looked down at Zarabeth's body. Then the grimy fingers touched the frozen cheek gently, and he stepped back and stood waiting.

Kirk drew his phaser, hesitated. It seemed inhuman to vaporize the body without a word. He touched McCoy's arm, and the two of them walked over until they could look down at her. The Captain cleared his throat. "To whatever Being, Belief, or Ideal this person may have held in reverence, I commend her physical body." He paused. "I'm sure her spirit was welcomed long ago." Eyes stinging, he finished quietly, "I wish I had known her."

McCoy stirred. "She was a very courageous and beautiful woman."

There was a long silence. Kirk had released the safety and was about to fire his phaser when Spock's voice came out of the shadows. "She was all the warmth in this world." The Vulcan moved forward, phaser in hand. As Kirk and McCoy stepped back, he sighted carefully and fired. Platform and body glowed, expanding in a burst of incandescent glory.

For a moment Zarabeth was outlined by a white fire, then the cavern was empty save for the living.

Spock dropped his arm and stood quietly as they filed past him to the mouth of the tunnel. Kirk thought he'd never seen him look so Vulcan—then he saw the eyes.

Chapter VII

Zar stood, legs braced against the whip of the wind, gazing up at the Guardian and the stars above it, bright, unwinking, and close. Watching him, Kirk remembered his own first sight of alien stars—the awe, tightness in the gut, a shivery joy—and smiled. The younger man hesitantly touched the time portal, and looked at the central portion, which was clear. As Kirk and McCoy joined him, he turned to them.

"How does it work, Captain?"

Kirk looked rueful. "A good question, with no answer. Some of the best minds in the Federation have studied it, and they can't agree. Ask Spock, he may have a theory. He was one of the ones selected to study it."

The bearded face frowned thoughtfully. "When I touched it, I sensed life—but not like any I ever felt before." He hesitated. "It . . . communicated. . . ." He shook his head, the frown deepening. "I can't explain it."

Kirk's eyes widened, "What do you mean, you—" He trailed off at Zar's emphatic headshake. They were interrupted suddenly by a now-familiar hail.

"Hey!" Doctor Vargas trotted into view. "You came back quicker than I—" she broke off, as she noticed the fourth member of their party. "You were successful!" Facing Zar, she looked up at him. "Greetings. I was expecting someone . . . younger."

Obviously confused, the younger man glanced at Spock, who stepped forward. "Doctor Vargas, this is Zar. We arrived at a later time period than we'd wished, and discovered an adult instead of the child we had anticipated. Zar, this is Doctor Vargas, head of the expedition that studies the time portal."

Shyly, the young man nodded a greeting. Vargas' gaze traveled over his clothing, obviously fascinated. "I'd like to talk to you before you leave, if you have the time. I've never seen leather clothing before that wasn't rotted with age in some ancient tomb. It's a wonderful opportunity for me to speak with someone who lived the way our ancestors did. Did you use gut for sewing? How did you tan the skins?"

Zar relaxed visibly at Vargas' matter-of-fact acceptance. "I used gut for sewing—my mother had some metal needles, but I made my own out of bone after they broke. I brought some things with me—would you like to see?"

The three officers watched for a moment as the young man and the archeologist examined the implements from the past, then Spock excused himself and left the group, heading for the camp building. He'd gone only a few steps when Zar caught him with a few swift strides and blocked his way. "I must speak with you for a moment . . . sir."

"Yes?" The Vulcan raised an inquiring eyebrow.

"I've been thinking about the powers of the Guardian." The gray eyes were level. "Now that I'm here, in the present, wouldn't it be possible for *me* to go back in time, also? Perhaps I could . . . be there to warn her, catch her before she fell. Save her before she died. If you could tell me how . . ."

Spock was shaking his head. "It isn't possible. What is *now*, must *be*. If you were to save her back then, you could not be here now, knowing she is dead. Language is inadequate to express the concepts involved. I can show you the equation later." Something touched his eyes for a moment. "I am truly sorry."

Disappointment flickered across the younger man's features for a second, then Zar nodded. The First

Officer looked over at Doctor Vargas, who was still examining the contents of the hide bundle. "Doctor Vargas—"

Vargas looked up. "Yes?"

"I must send a message by subspace radio. Is it possible to use the one at your camp?"

The plump little woman scrambled to her feet brushing ashy dust off the knees of her brown coverall. "Certainly, Mr. Spock. I'll show you where it is. As a matter of fact, perhaps you can help me with it. Our technician was injured last month in a fall while he was exploring the ruins, and had to be relocated to the nearest Star Base for treatment. We haven't received a replacement yet, and some of the circuits on the communications equipment don't seem to be working properly. Unfortunately, none of us is skilled enough to attempt repairs."

"Communications equipment is not my specialty but I will do what I can." The Vulcan turned back to Zar. "Go with the Captain and Doctor McCoy. They will show you a place to wash and provide you with more suitable clothing."

The younger man watched the First Officer leave, his expression wistful, before turning back to the others.

When they reached the camp building, Kirk departed in search of a spare coverall, and McCoy took his charge into the interior of the structure, noting the younger man's wondering glance at the furnishings. He handled himself with aplomb, however, until they reached the recreation/spare room. As they entered, lights automatically came on. Zar jumped, landed crouching, knife in hand, eyes darting from side to side.

McCoy put out a reassuring hand. "Take it easy son. The lights register body heat and turn on when we cross the doorway."

The gray eyes were still wide. "Automatically?"

"Yeah, come outside for a second."

They stepped back and the lights extinguished

McCoy's charge stepped in, cautiously, and gave a wordless exclamation when the lights flared back up. He spent the next minute determining just how much of his body was necessary to cause the phenomenon. (A leg was enough, but a foot wasn't apparently.)

The Doctor watched tolerantly, amused, and when the younger man had completed his experiment, introduced him to the marvels of indoor plumbing.

The shower facility finally caused his student to balk. "But water is to *drink*," he argued. "There can't be enough to waste like this!"

"We don't have to melt water, Zar. We can make as much as we want. There's plenty. How did you wash before?"

"In a bucket, sometimes. When my mother was alive, she made me wash more often, but lately—" One leather-clad shoulder moved in a slight shrug.

"Then it's about time you got a thorough scrubbing. I assure you it only hurts for a little while, and you're going to have to get used to it. This is primitive compared to the facilities aboard the *Enterprise*, and you'll be using them!" A smile twitched at the corner of his mouth at the look of apprehension on the younger man's face, and he forced himself to say sternly, "Now hurry up. The Captain will be back any minute. Remember, water controls here, soap there, warm air over on your right." Turning to leave, he cast a last glance at his unwilling pupil. "*In. Now.*" he ordered, and closed the door.

The sputtering sounds that ensued from behind the door assured him that his instructions were being followed. McCoy grinned, remembering that he should have warned Zar to hold his breath when he submerged his head.

Kirk entered the room, carrying a bundle of clothing. He cocked his head at the splashing noises. "Everything all right in there?"

"I assume so. He was a little dubious, but when I told him that everyone on a starship did it, he gave in. Where's Spock?"

"He went off to send that message. I think it's some sort of confirmation to T'Pau. Vargas told me he's fixing those circuits."

"He's probably glad of the excuse to stay away. Where's my medical kit?"

"I brought it." The Captain handed the black case over.

"Good." The Doctor took out several charges for his hypo. "Got to make sure he doesn't end up with every bug from measles to Rigellian fever. He probably has no natural immunities. Nice kid, isn't he? Friendly as a pup. I hate to think what a couple of weeks of Vulcan dehumanization is going to accomplish. Have you seen the way he watches Spock? He's already begun to imitate him."

"That's natural, isn't it? But I wouldn't worry too much. There's a lot of self-reliance there, and that'll help. He's got a lot of catching up to do, and Vulcan discipline may be just what he needs."

McCoy snorted. "The only lly Vulcan discipline is good for is—" He broke off as the sounds from the shower ceased.

Kirk grinned and headed for the door. "I'll leave you to get him dressed and barbered. After all, I'm a starship Captain—not a valet."

Zar had no sooner emerged from the shower, minus dirt and clothing, before the Medical Officer gave him several shots. "What's that for?" he wanted to know, tensing against the hiss of the hypospray.

"So you won't catch anything from us in the way of diseases. There, that's the last." McCoy ran his scanner, and a professional eye, over his patient. Although thin to the point of emaciation, the Doctor was pleased to see that the muscle tone was good. *Like a horse in racing form,* McCoy thought, *rather than a starvation case. Good-sized shoulders—when he reaches his proper weight, he'll mass more than Spock. How the hell did he get those scars?*

The jagged rips were long-healed, but still very noticeable. One ran along the right forearm, from wrist to elbow. The other began on the outside of the right thigh and continued nearly to the knee. McCoy shook his head at the thought of what the original wounds must've looked like.

"Where'd you get these, son?" he asked, indicating the ridged keloids.

"I was attacked by a vitha. She had cubs, and I took shelter next to her lair in a storm. I fell asleep, and she returned and was on me before I had time to feel fear at her."

The Doctor handed the younger man the clothes Kirk had provided, and as he helped with unfamiliar fastenings, continued, "What's a vitha? Was that one of the animals you painted?"

"No. They're very shy, and you seldom see them. Vicious when trapped, so I didn't hunt them, usually. Their wounds fester easily—as I discovered." He made shapes in the air. "About this tall, with big chests, and ears that—I could draw one, better than I can tell you."

McCoy picked up a stylus and a pad of paper, and demonstrated how to use them. The long, lean fingers with their ragged nails sketched quickly, and produced a picture of a bizarre creature that looked to the Doctor like a combination of otter and goat. He recognized it—he'd seen a skeleton in the book on Sarpeidon's past, and remembered it had been fully eight feet tall when balanced on its hind legs. "If that's what they looked like, you were smart to stay away from them." McCoy studied the hasty sketch further. The style was unsophisticated, but there was accuracy, and a suggestion of life and movement there. "I'll have to introduce you to Jan Sajii when we get back to the *Enterprise*. He's a pretty well-known artist, in addition to his work in xenobiology. Maybe he could give you a few pointers."

Zar nodded. "I'd like that."

McCoy took a pair of surgical scissors out of his med-kit, and motioned him to a chair. "It's almost a shame to cut this," he commented, hefting the black, slightly wavy mane that fell nearly to the younger man's waist. "But current male fashion—especially aboard starships—decrees that it's got to go." Solemnly, he draped Zar with a sheet, and began to clip briskly. "Used to be that a surgeon spent a lot of his time being a barber. Can't let the old-timers down."

His client looked confused. "Pardon?"

"Archaic reference. I'll explain later. Something you said a few minutes ago is bothering me. How could you 'feel fear' at the vitha? What does that mean?"

"It's what I tried to do to . . . Mr. Spock, when I thought you were going to find my cave. His mind was too strong for my fear. And three of you was too many to affect."

"You mean you can project your own emotions as a form of defense?"

"I don't know how I do it. If I'm frightened or angry, I can . . . focus my mind on a person or animal—if the animal is a higher life form—and I can make the fear and anger I feel go into the other mind. If I try hard, I can make the fear so strong that the animal will leave. The time the vitha attacked me, I was sure I was going to die, and my fear and anger as I struggled with her were so strong that I killed her. At least, that's what I think happened. I lost consciousness from the pain, and when I came to, she was dead—and my knife was still in its sheath. But I was never able to project that strongly again."

"Is this something you learned from Zarabeth?"

"No. She told me that some of the members of her family could sense emotions and communicate them to others, but she couldn't do it herself."

"What about reading thoughts—ideas?"

Zar thought for a careful moment before answering. "Sometimes, when you touch me . . . I can tell what you're thinking. Only a flash, then it's gone.

Today, when I was with others for the first time, I had to block it out, because the impressions were confusing. When I was small, I learned to tell what my mother was thinking, but she told me it wasn't polite to do that without her permission."

So, thought McCoy, *Zar may have inherited some of the Vulcan telepathic ability—in addition to whatever this fear projection is. Have to test him when we get back to the ship.* He busied himself with comb and scissors, and stepped back after a few more minutes to admire his handiwork. "Not bad. Now let's get rid of the beard."

A few minutes later, the younger man ran his hands over his head, then rubbed his chin. "I feel cold on my neck."

"That's not surprising," McCoy said absently, studying the newly revealed features. *I can see his mother there, in the jaw and mouth, but mostly . . .* He shook his head. "Come on," he said, gathering up the scissors. "Let's clean up, then we'll get something to eat."

The gray eyes lighted at the mention of food.

The kitchen was filled with appetizing odors when they arrived. Kirk and Spock were there ahead of them, sitting at the large table with Doctor Vargas and the rest of the archeologists. Zar hesitated just inside the door, suddenly conscious of all the eyes focused on him. Looking at more faces that he'd ever seen in his life, he felt his heart begin to slam, even though there was nothing to fight, nothing to flee. His eyes searched desperately for familiarity, found the Captain's face, and then Spock's, but there was no reassurance in their expressions—only shock.

McCoy put a hand on his shoulder, and Zar started at the touch. "Sit over here, son." The younger man was relieved to be moving, relieved to sit down next to the Doctor, escaping the stares he didn't understand. There was silence for a long moment, then Doctor Vargas cleared her throat.

"I didn't realize that family resemblances among

69

Vulcans were so marked, Mr. Spock. How are you two related?"

The First Officer's voice was normal, but he didn't meet the archeologist's eyes. "Family connections on Vulcan are complicated. The term is untranslatable."

There's another lie, thought McCoy, and glanced at Zar. The younger man stared at Spock, expressionless, but the Doctor knew that he'd picked up on the evasion, if not the reason for it.

The buzz of conversation started back up, and McCoy passed bowls of food to his protégé. Zar mentally compared the amount of food on the table with the number of people, and served himself only a small portion—he'd made do with less, many times. McCoy, noticing this, asked, "Aren't you hungry? There's plenty more where this came from."

"Enough for everyone?" The younger man looked skeptical.

"Sure. Go ahead—have as much as you want." McCoy passed him another bowl. Hesitantly, the young man served himself, then began to eat, slowly, handling the knife and fork efficiently, but mimicking the others at the table when it came to using the serving utensils. McCoy noticed that Zar copied Spock's choice of food.

When the meal was over, Doctor Vargas invited them to join the others in the recreation room, explaining that several of the archeologists played musical instruments, and they usually held an informal concert every evening.

As they found seats, Kirk whispered to McCoy, "You did that deliberately, Bones. Cutting his hair like Spock's, I mean."

The Medical Officer grinned, unrepentant. "Sure I did," he returned, "Spock can always use a little shaking up. Did you see his face when Zar walked in? No emotions, hell."

"It shook *me* up. I wonder what the reaction will be when we get back to the *Enterprise*?"

"They won't suspect the truth, because of the age

70

difference, but . . ." McCoy stopped, realizing that the concert was ready to begin.

The archeologists performed well, especially Vargas, who played the violin. Zar was enthralled by the music, McCoy saw. When the session ended, the younger man examined the violin with rapt attention, though he didn't venture to touch it. "How does it work?" he wanted to know.

Vargas smiled, and caressed the shining wood. "It would take me a long time to explain it all, Zar. Longer than you'll be here, because Mr. Spock says you'll be leaving on the supply ship tomorrow morning, But if you read up on violins, you'll be glad you got a chance to see this one. It's a genuine Stradivarius—one of about a hundred that still exist outside museums. I had to get a special permit to be allowed to keep it for personal use, and it took me years to save the money to buy it."

Spock, who had been sitting nearby, came over and studied the instrument. "A well-preserved example, Doctor Vargas. The tone is excellent."

"Do you play, Mr. Spock?" she asked.

"I did, at one time . . . but it has been years."

"By the way, thank you for repairing the communications device."

"It was no trouble. It needs a complete overhaul, however," The Vulcan turned to Zar. "I would like to talk to you for a moment."

When they reached the library, and privacy, Spock gestured the younger man to a seat. "It will not be easy to explain your presence when we reach the *Enterprise*." he began, without preamble. "Due to your . . . appearance, people will regard you as Vulcan, and expect certain behavior from you. I believe that the best course is for you to study Vulcan history and customs so that you'll know what's expected of you. I will begin teaching you the language as soon as you feel ready to learn."

He paused, then took out several microspools. "These will give you some basic information."

Zar couldn't think of anything to say, so he remained silent.

Spock raised an eyebrow. "You *can* read?"

"Yes." Zar replied shortly, stung. "My mother was a teacher, among other things, before she was exiled. Didn't you know that?"

The lean, saturnine face was remote. "No."

"She knew a lot about you . . ."

Spock stood up. "I see no logic in reviewing the past. When you've finished those tapes, I will set up a plan for your education. Good night."

After the Vulcan left, Zar continued to sit, uncertain of his next move. It had been a long day—was it only this morning he'd awakened on the ledge above the strangers' camp? He eyed the kitchen table, considered curling up underneath it. He would probably go unobserved—but perhaps it would not be polite. His eyes were beginning to close in spite of himself when McCoy found him.

"There you are. I came to show you where you can bunk tonight."

He followed the Doctor to the recreation room, where a sleeping bag was spread. "I'm afraid you'll have to make do on the floor, with the rest of us. It isn't often the archeologists have visitors, and there aren't many extra beds. These sleeping bags aren't too bad, though. They've got foam inserts, and heating controls." McCoy demonstrated. "So you shouldn't be too uncomfortable."

Zar was amused. "Doctor McCoy, last night I slept on a rock and ice ledge that was not much wider than I am, with nothing but my fur cloak for covering. I'll be fine here."

"I see your point. Well, good night, then." McCoy turned to leave, and on impulse, looked back. "Zar . . ."

"Yes?"

"Don't let Spock's . . . attitude bother you. That's just the way it is, with Vulcans."

The younger man shook his head ruefully, and

72

ghed. "I should have expected nothing else. My
other told me that he was cold and silent when she
rst met him, but that later, he was loving and gentle
her. He doesn't know me yet. I must prove my-
lf, as she did."

McCoy was startled, but recovered quickly. With
reassuring smile, he said good night again. Some-
ow he couldn't face the thought of sleep, so he went
tside.

With the cold wind lifting his hair, and the starlight
sy on his eyes, he paced slowly, considering. His
rst impulse had been to tell Zar the entire story of
e atavachron and its effect on the Vulcan's metab-
ism and reactions. Somehow, he couldn't bring
mself to disillusion the younger man . . . and Spock
ouldn't appreciate the interference. But still . . . he
ook his head, remembering the Vulcan's expres-
on as he looked at Zarabeth, just before they left
r behind, there in that icy inferno. Of course she'd
ll Zar about a different Spock than the one he'd
et today. *Loving and gentle . . . Damn. . . .*

McCoy leaned against the building, reflecting
imly that Zar's rescue was going to cause a lot
ore problems for the young man than it had solved.

Chapter VIII

The return trip aboard the supply ship was uneventf[ul]
and routinely boring for everyone—except Zar, wh[o]
spent hours staring at the stars through the viewpo[rt]
When he wasn't studying the tapes Spock had giv[en]
him, he was underfoot in the control cabin. The Fir[st]
Officer of the transport, a Tellarite female nam[ed]
Gythyy, took a shine to him, and began teaching hi[m]
the rudiments of piloting. Although he lacked t[he]
advanced mathematics necessary for the navigation[al]
computations, he proved adept at seat-of-the-pan[ts]
maneuvering.

When the *Enterprise* personnel disembarked, G[y]
thyy embraced her pupil roughly, after the custom [of]
her people, and turned to the three officers. "Th[at]
boy of yours is plenty smart. If the Federation does[n't]
want him, send him back to me. I could train hi[m]
to be the best pilot in the whole quadrant!"

As they walked down the loading ramp, Zar turne[d]
to Spock eagerly. "Did you hear her? She said—'[']

"Tellarites are notoriously given to overstat[e]
ment," the Vulcan said matter-of-factly.

Visibly deflated, Zar's voice was subdued. "I'[ve]
finished the tapes, sir."

Spock nodded. "I am designing a course of stu[dy]
for you that should allow you to attain the lev[el]
expected of a general studies university graduate. [I]
would not recommend specialization until you ha[ve]
completed it."

Doctor McCoy was busy explaining the order[s]

andemonium of Star Base 11 when Kirk and Spock returned from the administration offices.

Waving a clipboard of readouts, Kirk announced, Our clearance and bill of health. And new orders. axi duty, ferrying an experimental strain of honey-ee to Sirena, across this sector. Ever do any bee-eeping, Bones?"

McCoy shook his head. "No, can't say I've had ny contact with the little devils since I accidentally at on one at the Sunday School picnic when I was welve. I got the worst end of that deal!"

The two men laughed, and Zar asked, puzzled, What's a bee?"

An explanation of the life and habits of *Hymenop-ra Apis mellifera* (delivered by Spock) occupied em until they were beamed up to the *Enterprise*.

The Captain drew an appreciative breath, looking ound his ship. She was quiet, and still relatively eserted. He walked over to the transporter controls d flipped a couple, nodded his head at her quietly fficient hum. Glancing at the maintenance reports, e opened a channel.

"Computer," announced a mechanical-sounding male from the bulkheads around them. Zar jumped.

"Run a complete check on all systems, with spe-al emphasis on those that were overhauled. Give e a verbal report on general status and follow up ith a readout to be delivered to me when I key for

"Working," commented the voice. After a sec-nd's pause, it said, "All systems answer with an fficiency rating of plus 95 or better. Do you wish a reakdown by individual system?"

"Not at this time. I'll key for it in a few minutes. rovide copies upon request to Department Heads, Ir. Spock, and Chief Engineer Scott. Also dupli-tes to the maintenance authorities. Kirk out." He rned to Spock, who was standing beside him. "I ought I'd assign Zar to bunk in with some of the nmarried security men."

The Vulcan nodded. "That will be satisfactory."

McCoy joined them, directing their attention t
Zar, who had drifted over to the door of the trans
porter room and was experimenting with how clos
he had to stand to make it whoosh open. Grinning
the Doctor shook his head. "More curiosity in tha
one than a kitten. . . . I'm going to run some tes
on him today, blood pressure, heart, that sort c
thing. He needs some nutritional supplements, an
for that I'll need basal metabolism and some othe
readings. I can also test his intelligence—unless you'
rather do that, Spock."

The First Officer looked thoughtful. "I will nee
test scores in more specific areas, in order to assig
curriculum levels. However, I believe basic intell
gence and psychological testing is also in order. Suc
tests lack true scientific validity, but they provide th
best indicators yet developed."

McCoy was exasperated. "Does that mean yes, c
no?"

"Yes."

"Thank you. I'll need your help for one test I ha
in mind."

Spock's eyebrow climbed to his hairline. "M
help? Is that an admission of inadequacy, Doctor?

"Hardly, you—" McCoy sputtered, then controlle
himself with an effort. "I want to test his psi inde:
I think he's telepathic—and something else I've neve
encountered before. I'll need data from a trained tele
path before I can make any guesses."

The Vulcan looked thoughtful. "Now that yo
mention it, I recall that I was subject to some typ
of mental attack just prior to his appearance. . . ."

"He told me he was responsible for that. Called
'feeling fear.' I'll let you know when I need you."

The Captain beckoned to Zar, who joined then
"I've assigned you quarters with some men from th
security force. Spock will take you there. Then yo
can get something to eat—no, wait a minute. Bone
may want you to have an empty stomach. . . ."

76

The Doctor nodded, and Kirk continued, "He's going to give you a physical. A necessary evil . . . don't let it spoil that famous appetite. If you feel like a workout tonight, I'll see you in the gym at 1800 hours."

"Thank you, Captain."

The intelligence and psychological tests came first, then the thorough physical. By the time McCoy finished, Zar had worked up an immense appetite, and the Doctor was getting tired of explaining the reasons behind each test. Finally only the psi examination remained, and the Medical Officer signaled Spock to come to sickbay.

He turned to his patient, who was lying on the diagnostic table, his expression one of long-suffering restraint. "Buck up, Zar. Only one more test to go."

"Can I get something to eat now?" The younger man's tone implied that he was on the verge of fainting from hunger.

"Not yet. Spock's on his way down, and I want to try that mental projection trick of yours. You know, what you did with the animals, and us, to protect yourself."

"I may not have the strength," came the gloomy reply.

"Hello, Doctor!" The feminine voice came from the door of the examining room, and McCoy turned to see Christine Chapel, his Chief Nurse, and a physician in her own right.

"Good to see you, Chris." McCoy smiled. "You look rested."

"I had a terrific leave—bet I gained ten pounds. I'll have to—" Chapel caught sight of the man stretched on the examining table, and her blue eyes widened in shock as she took in the strangely familiar features. The Doctor waved a hand at his patient, who was gazing back at Chapel with undisguised pleasure. "Nurse Chapel, this is Zar. Zar, meet Nurse Chapel."

Chapel recovered her composure and smiled at the

77

young man, who sat up and saluted her carefully a∈ he'd read in the tapes. "Peace and long life, Nurse Chapel."

Her fingers moved to answer his salute, and she said warmly, "Live long and prosper, Zar."

McCoy caught Chapel's inquiring glance, and the raise of her eyebrow, but didn't enlighten her further—frankly because he couldn't think how to answer the unvoiced question. Instead he said, "Now that you're here, Nurse, you could help me. I'm testing Zar. I'll tell you what to do in a moment. Please sit over there."

The gray eyes followed the woman's every movement. The Doctor lowered his voice. "Zar—you're hungry, aren't you?"

"You know that already."

"Good. I want you to project what you're feeling at Nurse Chapel." The younger man looked back at the woman again, as the Medical Officer, on impulse, flicked the diagnostic field back on. He noted the dilation of the pupils, the jump in respiration and blood pressure, and poked his patient sternly. "Not *that* kind of hunger, son. I mean the kind in your stomach."

Zar looked confused, then his eyes narrowed in concentration. A few seconds went by, then Chapel looked up. "Doctor—I can't explain this, but suddenly I'm so hungry . . . starving . . . and I just ate!" She looked across the room and realization dawned. "Is *he* doing that?" Her eyes were suddenly filled with clinical fascination. "Mental projection of strong emotions? That certainly isn't a Vulcan talent."

They all turned as they heard the outer door to sickbay, and Spock entered the room. Chapel's gaze swept appraisingly from one alien face to another, but her expression remained carefully indifferent.

The Vulcan hesitated, then asked, "Have you met Zar, Miss Chapel?"

"Yes, Mr. Spock." The tone was noncommittal.

78

The First Officer evidently decided that at least a partial explanation was preferable to wild speculation, and he gestured stiffly in the younger man's direction. "He is a . . . member of my family, who will be staying aboard the *Enterprise* for an undetermined amount of time."

Chapel nodded, then turned to McCoy. "Will you need me anymore, Doctor? I have an experiment going in the other lab that needs checking."

At the Chief Surgeon's shake of the head and thank you, she smiled again at Zar, who remembered just in time to keep from returning it, and left.

Zar's gaze followed her admiringly. "She's nice . . . and very beautiful."

For the next thirty minutes, Spock and McCoy tested Zar's emotional projections. They discovered that he could make both of them feel hunger, and when McCoy pinched a nerve in his arm, they could both feel the pain. With the Doctor supplying the emotional currents, they found that Zar could pick up and identify his output, even when the Medical Officer left sickbay. The younger man's ability reached for a considerable physical distance—although he complained that background emotional "noise" from the crew interfered.

"Since I've been with people, the feelings have become easier to pick up," he commented. "Now I have to block them out, or they make it hard to concentrate. It's the same with thoughts, only they're not as strong."

Spock's expression thawed a bit as he nodded comprehendingly. "On Vulcan, much of our early training is designed to strengthen our personal barriers—our mental shields—to prevent the constant intrusion. You seem to have developed a natural shield, and practice in the vedra-prah mental disciplines will help. I believe that with training you can develop the mind-linking and melding abilities. My background in telepathic teaching techniques is lacking, but I will do what I can."

79

As soon as the testing was completed. McCoy told Zar he could eat, supplementing the food with a high-calorie nutritional drink. Leaving him to his meal, the officers examined the test results in the Doctor's office.

"As I said before, he's in remarkably good shape, considering the life he's led. Incredible stamina—he could outlast any of us. I had him on that treadmill for twenty minutes and he wasn't beginning to work up a sweat, much less breathe hard. We already know he's strong, whether from the higher gravity and the environment, or Vulcan ancestry, it's anyone's guess. Good thing he's good-natured." McCoy ran his eyes down the test readout, rubbed thoughtfully at his chin.

"Vulcan genes must be dominant as hell. Internal makeup not too different from yours—hope I never have to operate on him. Hearing—exceptional. He's got the Vulcan inner eyelid, but his eyesight is barely outside the Human range. Blood type—" the Doctor grimaced. "Well, I hope he never needs a transfusion, because we'd never match it. Incredible mix—even the color, sort of a greenish gray. Don't ever let him give you a transfusion or platelets, although your plasmas are compatible, as far as that goes. His teeth are beautiful. Shows you what you get from a diet with virtually no sugars."

Spock leaned forward. "And the other tests?"

"Psychologically, he's pretty well-adjusted, considering he's lived alone for seven years. Naive and socially immature, lacking in communication skills—what else could you expect? But quite a realist—matter of fact, his stability index is higher than yours."

A raised eyebrow was the only comment.

"As for intelligence, I ran him through the basic Reismann profile they give the kids when they enter school . . . here are the results."

The Vulcan studied the readout for a few minutes, then handed it back to the Doctor with a curt nod.

"Is that *all* you have to say?" McCoy snapped, temper visibly fraying. "You know damn well this intelligence rating is remarkable—you could hardly hope for more!" The Doctor leaned across his desk, after a glance at the open door, lowering his voice to an angry hiss.

"I've been watching what's happening, and I don't like it. I know it's none of my business, but if you break that kid's spirit with your tight-jawed Vulcan logic, I'll—"

Spock stood up, raising a hand to stem the Doctor's tirade. "Thank you for conducting the tests, Doctor McCoy," he said remotely, formally.

McCoy heard the Vulcan through the open door as he sat, clenched fists resting helplessly on the test results. "I'll show you where you will be staying. Follow me."

Zar's voice, eager, hesitant. "Were my tests . . . all right?"

"They indicated that if you apply yourself, you should reach satisfactory levels within a reasonable time. I'll show you where the library is, so that you can begin today. I've marked out the curriculum for you."

"Yes sir."

During his life alone on Sarpeidon, when blizzards had forced him to inactivity for weeks, Zar had formulated his own concept of paradise. There would be plenty to eat—as much as one wanted, anytime!—it would be warm and safe, there would be many books to read, and, most of all, there would be people to talk to. Seven weeks of "paradise" forced him to a reappraisal of his definition.

Most of the time he was too busy to wonder whether he was happy or not. The days went by in a blur—lessons, working out in the gym with Kirk, coaching from Spock in telepathic controls and abilities, and, in his free time, exploring the *Enterprise*. Zar had fallen in love with the starship, and Kirk,

81

recognizing a kindred emotion, let him indulge his passion. He was soon a familiar figure to the crew of each section, who responded to his interest by informally adopting him.

"I hope after we transfer these bees we'll be finished with milk runs for a while." Lieutenant Sulu commented to Zar after a week out.

"You mean honey runs, don't you, Sulu?" Uhura suggested, turning away from her communications panel. Sulu groaned.

The helmsman had been teaching his young friend basic battle tactics, using the computer-recorded log of the *Enterprise*. He keyed another sequence onto the navigation screen. "After we fired our main phaser banks, the outermost enemy ship took out our starboard deflectors. That left the Captain in a real mess, because the *Hood* was on our starboard side, and her maneuvering power was limited to auxiliary impulse. She couldn't defend us from the starboard side, and a direct hit would've crippled the ship."

The gray eyes studied the screen, and Zar nodded. "What did the Captain do?"

"He slapped a tractor beam on the *Hood* from the starboard side. That made the *Hood*'s deflector screens, which were still up, spread out so that we had limited deflection ability. Then we got the two remaining enemy ships when they came in for the kill. You see, they figured the *Enterprise* was going to try and run, towing the *Hood*. Instead, when they came within range, we took out the one on the port side with our photon torpedoes, and the *Hood* grazed the other with her phasers. That made it two to one, and the other ship took off. We lost her because the *Hood* had blown a seal and was losing pressure on two decks. We had to beam most of her personnel over to this ship, while the techs patched her up. Made for crowded living for about a week."

The bridge intercom came to life. "Lieutenant Sulu," Spock's voice said.

"Sulu here, sir."

"Is Zar on the bridge?"

"Yes, sir."

"Instruct him to join me in the library, I require his presence immediately. Spock out."

The helmsman turned to pass on the message, but the bridge doors had already snapped shut.

Sulu shook his head and looked at Uhura. "I sure don't envy him. Having our First Officer as an instructor in *one* subject is enough to drive you crazy. I know, I took a course in quantum physics he gave once. Picture having him personally supervising your entire education. . . ."

Uhura looked thoughtful. "He's pretty hard on him, but maybe that's the way Vulcans develop that stoic nature."

"Not according to what I've read. Most Vulcan families are extremely disciplined, but also very close-knit. Spock is more impersonal with Zar than with anybody else."

"I noticed something that may account for it. Have you ever looked at Zar's eyes?" Uhura leaned forward a little, lowering her voice.

"No—other men's eyes don't do anything for me, I'm afraid." Sulu grinned.

"They're gray. I never heard of a Vulcan with eyes that light before. I asked him once what exactly was his relationship to Spock."

"What did he say?"

"He got that remote look, and said that Vulcan family connections are extremely complex, and that he couldn't translate the exact term for it."

"He's probably right about that." Sulu looked thoughtful. "They must be fairly closely related, though, for such a marked resemblance. If I didn't know Spock has no brothers, I'd wonder."

"There's something funny about the whole thing, light eyes and all. I'll bet that Zar is part Human, and that Spock is hard on him because of it."

"If you're right, then that's an illogical attitude for our First Officer to have, considering that . . ."

83

The helmsman broke off abruptly and turned back to his console, as the bridge doors opened and the Captain entered. "Report, Mr. Sulu?"

"All systems normal, sir. Proceeding on course, warp factor four."

Zar was aware of the speculation that surrounded his relationship to the Vulcan, of course. It was impossible for him *not* to know. His innate telepathic ability, nourished by the ancient mind-linking techniques, grew until he could communicate freely with the First Officer. Freely, that is, to the extent that he could draw upon the logical, fact-containing areas of that brilliant mind. His knowledge of the Vulcan language increased geometrically with each teaching session. He could tap the first level, refreshing in its chill precision, its relentless clarity, as beautiful and uncluttered as pure mathematics. The first level, nearly devoid of personality, of everything that the younger man craved with a longing that went unacknowledged, almost unsensed. The first level—and guarding it, like a barrier, the mind-shield.

Somehow that intangible wall became his enemy. It hovered at the back of each contact, reminding the younger man that he knew almost nothing about the remote stranger who was so different in flesh than he'd been in dreams. The mind-shield stood between them, barring any closeness, any sharing, and his hate for it, irrational as he knew it to be, grew with each session.

Spock sensed the growing tension in the younger man's mind, but ignored it—almost to his undoing. They were linked, fingers to temples, solid blocks of knowledge-impressions flowing from one mind to the other, when he felt Zar's communication fade, realized the younger man had dropped his shield. Hastily Spock pulled back, clamping his own barrier tighter, refusing the implied offer to meld, rejecting any deeper contact. Before he could break away, he felt it come, a solid wave of confused emotion that battered at his shield. Zar's communication, a barrage as incoherent and nonverbal as it was raw and powerful, shook the Vulcan, hurt him on a level that was emotional as well as mental. For a moment they were *one,* and there was pain, only pain.

Spock shook his head violently, fighting the pressure of Zar's fingers even as they slackened. He stumbled back a pace, and stood swaying a little, to face the other. Their quick breathing was the only sound in the room.

The younger man's face was ashen. "I'm sorry. I didn't realize—I was only trying to—" he gestured helplessly.

The Vulcan could feel the memory of the pain rasping his throat as he spoke. "On Vulcan, what you attempted just now is regarded as a heinous crime. Forcing a meld is an unforgivable invasion of the spirit."

Zar nodded impassively, but Spock could feel his remorse—hear it in his voice. "I know that, now. I acted on impulse . . . it was wrong. I'm sorry."

The pain was fading, leaving behind only a physical shadow—a headache. Spock could feel the pressure behind his eyes, pounding, and his voice was harsher than he'd intended. "See that you remember. If you do not, I can't continue training you."

The gray eyes narrowed. "I suppose you *could* call it training, as if I were an animal. But I think it's closer to the programming you do to the computers." His expression changed, and he half-extended his hand. "I can't *touch* you. *Why?*"

Anger welled, born of the pain, and the Vulcan remembered all the times he'd been asked that question, different words, but holding the same meaning. *Why,* he asked them all, Leila, Amanda, McCoy, and now this gray-eyed quasi-reflection . . . *why do you ask of me the thing I cannot give? I am what I am. . . .*

Even so, something within him wanted to answer that anguished query, but the ingrained reserve of years held. Quickly, before that something forced a response, he turned on his heel and left the room.

The same night, after a brisk workout on self-defense techniques with Kirk, Zar asked the Captain hesitantly if he might speak with him—privately.

He felt comfortable in Kirk's quarters immediately, though this was the first time he'd visited them. Somehow he'd never felt at ease in Spock's cabin— a reflection of the way he felt toward both men, Zar decided, studying the paintings with admiration.

Kirk pointed to a chair. "Sit down. Would you like some Saurian brandy?"

Zar eyed the bottle the Captain produced warily. "Is that ethanol?"

"Yes, it certainly is."

"No thank you, then. My roommates gave me some once, and it made me throw up."

The Captain cocked an amused eyebrow, and put the liquor away. "It's been known to do that, all right." He sobered. "What did you want to see me about?"

Zar didn't reply. His face was closed, and only the tightness of the jaw muscles betrayed him. Kirk had an uncanny feeling of *déjà vu*. The Captain sat back, waiting with an outward show of patience. Finally the younger man looked up. "You and Mr. Spock have served together for some years now."

"Yes, we have."

"You know him better than anyone else. He trusts you, and you trust him. If you feel that you're betraying that trust by talking to me, I want you to tell me."

"That's fair enough. Go on."

With an abrupt gesture, Zar straightened, one clenched fist grinding into his other palm. His voice was harsh, demanding. "Why doesn't my father like me?"

Kirk sighed, realizing he should have expected something like this. Zar continued in a rush of words,

"I've studied—McCoy says I learn faster than anyone he's ever known. I've done everything I can to learn how to be Vulcan. I've followed the dietary restrictions. No meat. My mother told me how kind and loving he was. How gentle. When I was small, I used to dream about him, how he came from the stars, and I used to imagine that he'd come and take me with him someday. She used to say that if my father could see me he'd be proud of me. . . ."

The Captain sighed again, then sat back, eyes level. "I'm going to tell you the truth, because I think it's your right to know," he said slowly. "When he went back in time through the atavachron, something strange happened to Spock. He changed—whether the change was caused by the device, I can't say. Since it didn't happen when we went back using the Guardian, it probably was. While he was with . . . your mother, Spock became like the Vulcans of that time period—5,000 years ago. He . . . reverted . . . became an emotional being. One with strong feelings. He did things he'd never done before, even to eating meat."

"And while he was this way . . . he . . . took my mother." It was a statement. Zar took a deep breath, shook his head. "Then it wasn't love he felt for her, only . . ." he swallowed, then swallowed again, and his voice was thick. "Poor Zarabeth. All her life, she remembered a dream, something that was never real. She never realized that she was . . . used."

Kirk put a hand on the younger man's shoulder, shook it a little. "We don't know that's true. The only person who knows is Spock, and I doubt he'll ever discuss it. It could be that your mother found something in him that they made real between them. That's really none of your concern. I told you what I know, so you'd understand that Zarabeth told you the truth—her truth. What was true for her, doesn't necessarily hold true for you, now."

The gray eyes held only bitterness. "He meant it, when he said it was because of duty that he searched for me. He doesn't want me—never did. I was stupid not to realize it."

"He risked his life—and more, he allowed McCoy and me to risk our lives—to find you."

"Not because he *wanted* to, though. So many things are clear, now, that I didn't understand before. I'm an embarrassment to him—a . . . barbarian that happens to look like him. Every time he sees me he's reminded of an incident he'd rather forget. No wonder he won't discuss his family on Vulcan with me. Vulcan customs are old, and strict. Offspring like me are called 'krenath.' It means 'shamed ones.' You Humans also have a word. Bastard."

While Kirk was still searching his mind for something—anything—to say, Zar nodded gravely and left.

Chapter IX

Doctor McCoy halted outside the quad that Zar shared with two other men, and keyed the door panel. It opened, and he stepped in to see Juan Cordova and David Steinberg, Zar's roommates, playing poker in the sitting room the three shared. Cordova looked up. "Hi, Doc." He nodded at the bedroom. "He's in there.

"Thanks, Juan," the Doctor hesitated. "You seen much of him lately?"

Steinberg shook his head. "Not for the last couple of days. He's been keeping to himself."

Cordova looked worried. "I even broke down and asked him if he wanted to join us in a hand, and he turned me down. First time *that's* happened."

In spite of his concern, McCoy's mouth twitched. "He plays a pretty mean game of poker, doesn't he? Taught him everything I know—till it got too damn expensive."

Steinberg was disgusted. "You mean *you're* the one we should blame? That's the last time I play poker with a Vulcan!"

"Yeah," Cordova agreed. "I'm taking him with me next time I get leave—we'll clean up every casino from the Center to the Klingon Empire!"

The Medical Officer chuckled, then sobered. He gestured at the closed door. "Do you know of any reason—have you done anything that might—"

Steinberg was shaking his head. "You mean have we corrupted him lately, the answer is no. When I came right out and asked him if he was all right, he just looked at me and said, 'Of course. Do I appear any different?' And he said it—you know how . . . Vulcan."

McCoy grimly keyed the door panel. "I know indeed." he muttered.

"Who is it?" Zar's voice, but the door stayed closed.

"McCoy."

The panel slid open. "I'm sorry, Doctor. I didn't know you were there. Please come in. . . ." The younger man sat before an easel, a brush and palette in his hand.

"Haven't seen much of you for the last couple of days, Zar. What's up?"

Zar dabbed carefully at the canvas, not meeting the Doctor's measuring stare. "Up? The *Enterprise* maintains a constant gravity of one Earth gee. Why should—"

"Not another one!" McCoy interrupted with a groan. When the artist didn't raise his eyes from the canvas, he amended, "I meant, what kind of things have been going on with you lately?"

One shoulder twitched in what the Medical Officer assumed was a shrug. Baffled, McCoy walked around to get a better look at the painting.

It showed a blood-colored sun setting over a jagged upthrust of rock and ice. The background was muted, and the glow of the sun on the ice-glazed boulders was a scene McCoy remembered vividly. The defiant angle of the glacier stabbed the roundness of the sun like a dagger.

"Cold as hell, in spite of the sun," the Doctor commented. "I remember how strange that icy glow looked. You've really caught it here."

Some of the remoteness left the artist's expression at the compliment. Zar dabbed carefully at one corner again, turning so McCoy couldn't see his face, but his voice betrayed him. "It's beautiful. So cruel, but beautiful. I miss it . . . sometimes." He straightened, laid down the brush. "This is Jan's favorite."

"You've done others?"

"Yes, I like to paint almost everything I've seen. I've done three others since I came on board, and some sketches."

"I'd like to see them."

Zar dragged several canvases and a fat sketchbook out of the cabinet built into the bulkhead. "I'm afraid they aren't the same as they were in my head," he apologized. "Nothing comes out the way I envision it."

McCoy set the first painting on the other side of the easel, and examined it. A portrait of Jan Sajii—the distinctive features were unmistakable, despite the flaws in perspective. The artist had caught the characteristic tilt of the head, the humor in the eyes. He could see Sajii's influence in the style. "That's the first one I did," the younger man offered. The Medical Officer nodded.

"That's old Jan, all right. You've really caught him."

The second painting was a posed grouping, showing Spock's Vulcan harp propped against a chair, next to an open book. Mathematical equations showed on the pages. A Star Fleet uniform tunic hung over the back of the chair, with one sleeve dangling free. Gold braid of a full commander winked against the blue. McCoy studied the picture intently, nodding to himself, then looked back at Zar, who didn't meet his eyes. He lifted the painting down carefully.

The last canvas was an abstract, with swirling shades of purple, muting into lavender, shading out to rose and light blue. A jagged slash of black jumped out of the center to drip off the side of the painting. It disturbed McCoy. "What's this one?" he asked.

The gray eyes still avoided his. "I painted it the other night. It really doesn't mean anything."

The Doctor made a rude noise. "Like hell it doesn't mean anything. I'll bet a psychologist would have a good time with it. Wish I had more training in that field." He opened the sketchbook as Zar put the pictures away, smiling a little as he recognized himself, bent over a microscope in the lab. The sketches varied from people aboard the *Enterprise* to Sarpeidon's now-extinct animals, with some conventional pen-and-inks of fruit and a few draftsman-like studies of electronic circuitry. The Doctor found himself turning back to one of Uhura bending over her communications panel, dark head tilted characteristically as she listened to voices only she could hear. "I really like this one."

The younger man looked over his shoulder, then, taking the book from McCoy deftly ripped the page out and handed it to him. The Doctor grinned, pleased, and pointed to the corner. "Thanks. Can you sign it for me? I've got a feeling that'll be worth money some day. Jan agrees with me—says you've got real talent."

Zar shook his head, mumbling, "You're an optimist, Doctor," but McCoy could tell he was pleased as he signed the sketch with a flourish.

Though still puzzled by the younger man's reticence and ill-humor, the Medical Officer was relieved that his black mood seemed to be lifting. He suggested lunch, and saw a glint of humor in the gray eyes. "Have you *ever* known me to refuse food?"

The small galley was crowded when they entered. McCoy punched in his order, and took a sandwich, soup, coffee and a large piece of pie to an empty table. His companion joined him in a minute, carrying a tray loaded to its edges with a huge salad, soy protein wafers, several vegetables and two kinds of dessert. The Doctor shook his head, watching the other tackle the salad enthusiastically. "You still taking that supplement I prescribed?"

"Yes. It tastes good."

"Well, I think you can stop soon. You've certainly filled out since you left Sarpeidon."

"I know. I had to get a size larger coverall the

other day. The old one got to be too small in the shoulders."

"Keep eating like that, and it'll be too small around your waist."

Zar paused, bite halfway to his mouth, and looked slightly alarmed. "Do you really think so? I work out with Captain Kirk almost every day, and by myself a lot. The Captain says it makes him tired to watch me." He put his fork down, shaking his head. "I wouldn't like being fat."

McCoy grinned. "Don't be so literal. Go on, eat your food. I was kidding—that means making a joke. Just come up to sickbay sometime and let me put you on the scale for my records—and to satisfy my curiosity."

The conversation had turned again to painting, and McCoy was telling his listener about the art galleries on Earth when all animation abruptly faded from Zar's eyes. The Doctor followed his gaze to see the First Officer and the Chief Engineer across the mess-room. *Now we'll find out what this is all about,* he thought, waving them over.

The two officers sat down, and McCoy and Scott exchanged a few comments, while Spock and Zar sat silently. The Doctor looked from one impassive face to the other. *Worse than ever. And Zar isn't trying anymore.*

"Have you finished your physics assignment?" The Vulcan was abrupt; his inflection that of a teacher to a backward student. McCoy could sense Zar's embarrassment, though the younger man's face didn't change.

"Most of it, sir."

"Very well. What are Fraunhofer lines?"

Zar sighed. "The dark absorption lines in the solar spectrum."

"Essentially correct, but lacking in detail. What is the function of spectroscopy?"

"It was through the function of spectroscopy that . . ." Zar continued, his voice precise, sounding like a study tape. He finished, and took a deep breath.

The catechism continued. "What is the Heisenburg Uncertainty Principle? You need not give the math."

Generous bastard, McCoy thought, glancing at the Vulcan. *Why is he doing this?* Sudden flash of insight: *he doesn't know any other way to talk to the kid. . . .*

". . . the measurement of its moment is approximately equal to Planck's constant, 'h.' 'h' is equal to 6.26 times 10 to the minus 27th ergs per second," Zar finished with relief.

Stop. Now. McCoy thought. But the Vulcan continued after a second's pause, "What laws govern photoelectric effect, and explain the phenomenon using the concepts of quantum theory."

The younger man hesitated for a long moment. His answer this time was slower, broken by pauses as he dredged the information out of his memory.

When the three laws had been duly given, McCoy turned to the Vulcan to change the subject, but Spock ignored him. "The formula, please."

The gray eyes flicked to the Doctor's face, then dropped. Zar's voice this time was lower, as though the muscles in his throat were constricting, and he hesitated between words, obviously groping. Finally he stumbled through.

The First Officer raised an eyebrow. "You need to review that. Very well, what is meant by the critical angle of incidence?"

Long pause. McCoy found he was gripping the handle of his spoon as he stirred his now-cold coffee. The younger man thought intently, then his face hardened and his chin came up. "I don't know, sir."

"The critical angle of incidence . . ." began Spock, and proceeded to lecture capably for the next four or five minutes. The Doctor glanced over at Scotty, who was listening with a credible amount of polite interest for one who had heard it all before.

Finally the lecture seemed to be drawing to a close. Spock finished with a two-sentence summary of the topic, and stopped. Zar looked at the other two officers, paused for a beat, then slowly raised an eyebrow. "Fascinating," he intoned.

The imitation was perfect, but there was nothing good-natured about it. *There is mimicry, and there is mockery, and this,* thought McCoy, *is definitely mockery.* It wasn't lost on the Vulcan, who dropped his eyes, hastily picking up his fork.

The Doctor cleared his throat. "What do you think our next assignment will be Scotty?"

"Whatever it is, I hope it'll be somethin' wi' a little excitement to it. I'm findin' more thrills in my technical journals than I'm encounterin' on this trip."

Conversation continued desultorily between the Chief Engineer and the Medical Officer, until Scotty announced that he had duty and departed.

Spock, who was evidently finding the atmosphere uncomfortable, made another attempt. "I've finished reviewing your current assignment in biochemistry, Zar. Your answers were accurate, for the most part. If you have your next assignment ready I could—" Without a word, the younger man got up and left the table, heading for the food processors on the other side of the galley.

Embarrassed and concerned, McCoy attempted a light tone. "Never saw anyone with an appetite like that! He'd put Attila and all his Huns to shame!" Zar returned to the table with a large, meat-filled sandwich. Deliberately, he picked it up and began eating, ignoring everything around him.

When the Doctor was relating the incident to Kirk, later that day in sickbay, the Captain smiled at that point. McCoy shook his head. *"It wasn't funny, Jim. Zar ate it right in front of him. It was the worst insult he could give. You should have seen him—and you should have seen Spock!"*

"Really bothered him?"

"Yeah. He got that look—you know the one, when he's hurt and he won't show it—and left. Zar just sat there until he was out of sight, then dropped the food, and got out of there. I don't mind telling you I'm worried about both of them. What could've caused Zar to do such an about-face?"

Kirk looked uneasy. "I think I know. I told him the truth the other day—about Spock, and the atavachron, and his relationship to Zarabeth."

The Doctor whistled softly. "That could explain it—he took it really hard?"

"Yes. This is serious. I can't risk allowing this kind of thing to affect Spock's efficiency. He's too valuable an officer. I feel sorry for Zar, but—hell, I feel sorry for Spock, too. But I've got a starship to run. This can't go on."

The bosun's whistle filled the air. "Captain Kirk acknowledge, please," came Lieutenant Uhura's contralto.

He thumbed a button on the sickbay communicator. "Kirk here."

"Captain, I have a Priority One distress call, from sector 90.4. It's in code, sir. For your eyes only."

"On my way." Kirk was out the door before McCoy was out of his seat.

Chapter X

The bridge doors slid open, and before Kirk stepped through, Uhura placed a coded readout in his hand. Sitting down, he flipped a switch on his command chair.

"Computer."

"This is Captain Kirk. Do you have voice-print ID?"

"Identity acknowledged."

"Lieutenant Uhura received a Priority One distress call with accompanying message. Scan, decode and translate to a readout, then erase the translation from your memory banks after I've received it."

"Working."

He sat tensely, resisting the urge to drum his fingers on the arm of the command chair. The bridge crew cast covert glances at him, but the Captain was oblivious, mind racing. Priority One from Sector 90.4 was ominous. That sector held only one thing of any importance—the Guardian of Forever.

A strip of readout spouted under his fingers. The translation read:

PRIORITY ONE

Stardate:	6381.7
From:	NCC 1704, Starship *Lexington*, Commodore Robert Wesley, Commanding
TO:	NCC 1701, Starship *Enterprise*, Captain James T. Kirk, Commanding

CURRENT ASSIGNMENT: Patrol of sector 90.4, code name, Gateway.

PROBLEM: Have picked up blips of three vessels at extreme range of subspace scanner, have identified intruders as originating from sector RN-30.2, Romulan Neutral Zone.

TENTATIVE IDENTIFICATION: Romulan warships.

ESTIMATED TIME OF CONTACT: 10.5 hours.

EVALUATION: Military engagement probable. Request immediate assistance.

MAYDAY—DISTRESS—MAYDAY—DISTRESS—MAYDAY—

Kirk too three deep breaths, closing his eyes, ordering his thinking. Straightening, he addressed Ensign Chekov, who was watching him expectantly. "Present course, Mr. Chekov?"

"Two-nine-zero mark five, sir."

"Change course to seven-four-six mark six."

"Aye, sir. . . ." Chekov turned to his panel, turned back after a short pause. "Course laid in, sir."

"Helm, ahead warp factor eight, Mr. Sulu."

The almond-shaped eyes widened, and Sulu made an adjustment. The barely perceptible vibrations of the ship suddenly increased. The *Enterprise* hummed. Kirk began counting seconds in his head. He'd reached eleven when the intercom flashed. Flipping the channel open, he smiled grimly. "Yes, Mr. Scott?"

The intercom was silent for a long moment, as Chief Engineer Scott evidently wondered if his Captain had developed telepathy. Finally, he spoke, voice subdued, "Captain. I suppose you've a good reason for taxin' m' poor engines like this?"

"A very good reason, Mr. Scott."

"Aye, sir." The Chief Engineer must have looked

at his stress readouts, because he said, "How long will we be runnin' at this ungodly speed, sir?"

"About twelve hours, Mr. Scott. We'll alternate with warp nine whenever the engines will take it."

There was a long, reproachful silence, then a sigh. "Aye, sir."

In spite of his anxiety, Kirk smiled. "Hold 'er together, Scotty. I'm calling a briefing in five minutes. Main briefing room. Kirk out."

He heard the doors to the bridge, then Spock was standing beside him. The Vulcan ran a quick eye over the helm controls, and turned to him, inquiring without words.

Kirk nodded. "We've got a problem, Mr. Spock." He handed the readout to the First Officer, who scanned it with a steadily ascending eyebrow. The Captain turned to Uhura. "Contact Doctor McCoy and inform him of the briefing. I'll see you in the main briefing room in three minutes. Spock, with me."

The room was hushed as Kirk summarized the situation, concluding. "We have an unusual problem here. We in this room made up the landing party that discovered the Guardian, and know its capabilities as a time portal. Therefore I caution you to remember that, to our crewmates, we are assisting the *Lexington* because of unauthorized Romulan entry into our space—and that's *all*. No other crew member of either ship must learn about the Guardian. That includes Commodore Wesley and his officers. Is that clear?" Nods rippled around the table. "Good. I speculate that the entry of three vessels represents a scouting force only. Any other ideas?"

Spock steepled his fingers, then said slowly, "Captain, Romulan battle tactics are far from crude. These ships may be a diversionary force—masking the arrival of a fleet."

Scotty was nodding. "Aye, sir. It'd be a good idea t' increase th' patrol along th' Neutral Zone. At least that way, we'd have some warnin' if we have t' face a larger force."

Kirk looked thoughtful. "Lieutenant Uhura, send a complete report of the situation—including Mr. Scott's advisement—to Star Fleet Command. Refer to the Guardian by the planet's code name, Gateway. Send the message to Admiral Komack, code 11."

"Aye, sir."

"Mr. Scott, instruct the helm to go to yellow alert. Dismissed. Spock, please remain."

The briefing room emptied rapidly.

The Captain looked at the Vulcan bleakly. "Any ideas, Spock?"

"Insufficient data at this time—as you well know, Captain."

"Yes, I do know. It would be safer to holler for help throughout Star Fleet—but the secrecy surrounding the Guardian forbids that. After all, two starships ought to be able to handle three Romulans without any trouble. It'd arouse a lot of suspicion if I called in the cavalry over a burned-out sun and a few burned-out planets—one of which has a small archeological dig."

"As soon as Admiral Komack receives your communication, he will detail sufficient strength to this sector—he has the authority you lack."

"I only hope we're not too late. . . . When I remember what one man did back in time, unintentionally, I shudder when I think about what the Romulans could do deliberately. The past is so damn fragile—which reminds me of something I've been wanting to talk to you about. What's to become of Zar?"

The Vulcan looked blank. "What do you mean, Captain? Elucidate, please."

"I mean that I've kept quiet and let him stay aboard the *Enterprise* until he became somewhat adjusted to modern society. It wouldn't have been fair to him to turn him loose in a world he couldn't cope with—nor would it have been fair to our society to turn Zar oose on it, I'm afraid!" Kirk grinned, remembering the younger man's first weeks aboard ship. "However, he's caught up remarkably, and the fact remains that he's a civilian. And, no matter how peaceful our intentions, this is still a military vessel—especially now. So what are your plans for him—assuming we get out of this?"

Spock considered for a long moment. "I don't know, Captain. You are right, of course. It is against regulations for him to remain aboard the *Enterprise*."

"What about Vulcan? You could take him yourself. You've still got enough leave for five men. Then he could stay with your parents—"

Spock was shaking his head. "No. Zar would be at a disadvantage on Vulcan. The climate, for one thing. The thin air, the heat, would make adjustment difficult."

"As I recall, the air was pretty thin back there in that ice age. He's healthy—he'd get used to the heat."

"He'd need constant attendance and guardianship. Vulcan has an old, custom-ridden culture. He speaks the language, but he is not prepared for the social structure. It would be . . . extremely difficult."

"I don't think you're giving him enough credit. He'd adjust. I think it'd be just as difficult—maybe more—for you."

Spock looked up. Kirk nodded. "Difficult for you, because there's walking, talking proof that you're not infallible. Difficult for him, because he's krenath."

The Vulcan's eyes narrowed. "Where did you hear that word?"

"Zar mentioned it once. Said it means 'shamed ones.' Also, 'bastard.' "

The First Officer's eyes were hooded, unfathomable, his face an alien mask that Kirk had seen only once or twice before. "Zar doesn't understand the semantic content. Nor do you."

The Captain stood up. "Well, a discussion of semantics was not what I had in mind when I brought the subject up. I just wanted you to be aware that

101

the change will have to be made. When we go to yellow alert, tell him he's confined to quarters—no, tell him to report to McCoy, in sickbay. That's the best-shielded part of the ship, and Bones may need help in handling wounded, if there's a fight."

Spock raised an eyebrow. "If? Hostilities seem likely, Jim."

"I'm afraid you're right."

Zar was confused and excited. He'd awakened from a restless sleep to find a message flashing on the screen in his quarters. Now, in response to Spock's orders, he hurried through the corridors toward sickbay. The ship was strangely deserted, and a yellow light flashed from each signal panel. A contingent of security personnel, including his friend David, passed him at a dead run, as though he were invisible.

Sickbay was a scene of furious activity. Doctor McCoy, Nurse Chapel and the other medical personnel were checking and sorting supplies, and rigging temporary cots in the labs. McCoy looked up and saw the younger man standing hesitantly in the doorway. "Zar—glad you're here. Go into the storage area and lug that old-fashioned coronary stimulator and the battery resuscitator into that corner there. If we lose power we may need them."

The Chief Surgeon kept all of them scrambling for the next two hours, then straightened, looking around the transformed sickbay, and addressed his staff. "Guess that's all we can do for now. Report back when we go to red alert. Zar, you stay here."

When they were alone, the younger man looked wonderingly at the preparations. "What's going to happen?"

"You mean nobody told you?"

"No, Mr. Spock just told me to come here and help you any way I could."

"Well, Spock's got a lot of things on his mind, I guess. We've received a distress call from the *Lex-*

ngton, another Federation starship. She reported un-authorized entry of Romulan vessels into our space. When you're talking about Romulans, that generally means an act of war."

"War? You mean the *Enterprise* is going to fight?" The gray eyes gleamed.

"Probably, and don't get any ideas about going up to the bridge. The Captain would toss you out on your pointed ear. You're staying down here, where you'll be out of the way. I can use those muscles of yours to help if there are casualties."

"When will we fight?"

"I don't know. We'd better get there soon, or our engines will burn out, and our first patient will be Scotty."

"And I have to stay *here?* There's nothing to see!"

McCoy sighed. "Bloodthirsty, aren't you? Get this straight, Zar. There is absolutely *nothing* glamorous or thrilling about *any* war, and interstellar conflicts are no exception. You'll realize that when you see your friends coming through that door—horizon-tally."

"I've heard of the Romulans, but very little. They're deadly and brutal enemies, according to what I've read. What are they like?"

McCoy's grin was sardonic. "Go look in the mir-ror."

"They're *Vulcans?*"

"Not exactly. An offshoot of the parent stock that went their separate way long before Vulcans adopted their philosophy of peace and total objectivity. The Romulans are what the Vulcans were long ago—un-principled and warlike. As far as we know, their culture is a kind of military theocracy. Not too unlike the ancient Spartans of Earth's history."

Zar nodded absently, suddenly withdrawn. "I've read of them. 'With your shield or on it.' Like the Japanese culture of the early twentieth century on Earth."

McCoy's eyes had narrowed, watching him.

"There was something about what I said just now that you didn't like." He rubbed thoughtfully at his chin. "Let's see . . . could it be the reference to the nature of Vulcans in the remote past? Say, 5,000 years ago?"

The Doctor didn't miss the barely perceptible start quickly replaced by a carefully neutral mask. The younger man twitched a shoulder in that annoying half-shrug. "I don't know what you're talking about."

"The hell you don't. You're a worse liar than Spock. Jim told me he talked with you. I can imagine what you're thinking about your father, but—"

"I'd rather not discuss it." Zar interrupted. McCoy had seen that expression before, silent, stubborn, distant. It had plagued him for years on another face, and it angered him now.

"You acted like a ten-year-old today in the mess hall. God knows, I'm not usually put in the position of defending Spock, but you shouldn't have insulted him, especially in front of me and Scotty. *Grow up.* Whatever happened back in that ice age on Sarpeidor has nothing to do with—"

"I said, I don't want to discuss it!" The gray eyes were beginning to shine queerly, and the big hands with their lean, sinewy fingers clenched and unclenched. Against his will, McCoy found himself remembering how hard similar hands had felt as they locked themselves around his throat, felt again the damp rock of the cave wall against his back. A stir of fear (remembered, or present?) touched his spine like an icy splinter.

In spite of the fear—or because of it—McCoy felt his eyebrow climb, and heard the old cynical edge in his voice. "I've got a real talent for provoking supposedly logical, unemotional beings, don't I? Or is it that they just can't stand to hear the truth about themselves?"

Zar's mouth tightened, then his shoulders sagged and he nodded wearily. "You're right. I'm sorry about what happened. I wish I could tell him so, but he'd just *look* at me, and I'd feel confused and stupid all over again. It's like trying to move a mountain with your hands, and it'll never be any different." He shook his head. "As soon as the *Enterprise* makes port, I've got to leave."

"Leave?" The Doctor forced a calm he didn't feel, realizing suddenly how much he'd miss the younger man. "Where would you go?"

The gray eyes measured his concern, softened. "I've been thinking about it. I need a place where I can stand by myself, on my own. A place where what I am, the things I know how to do, would be needed, not a handicap. Maybe on one of the frontier planets . . ." Something touched the corners of his mouth that wasn't a smile. "I'll let you know where. You're almost the only one who would care—*he* certainly wouldn't."

"You're wrong. After all, he—"

"Found me." Zar interrupted wearily, nodding. "The simple fact of my existence mattered to him. *I* don't. There's only one person Commander Spock cares deeply for, and that's . . ." He trailed off as though remembering that he was speaking aloud. A muscle twitched in his jaw, and he finished, very softly, "Not me."

McCoy dared to put out a hand, touch the rigid shoulder. "Give it time, son. It's even harder for him than it is for you. Parenthood is never simple—even if you come to it in the usual fashion, much less have it dropped in your lap. It's *not* easy—I should know, I've made a pretty botched job of my attempt."

"You?" Zar looked up. "What do you mean?"

"I was married . . . for a while. I've got a daughter named Joanna. She's about your age."

"Where is she?"

"She's in medical school. She took nurse's training, then decided to specialize, and went back for her M.D. I've got a picture of her I'll show you, sometime. She's pretty—takes after her mother, fortunately."

Zar was interested. "Is she like you . . . nice, I mean?"

McCoy chuckled. "She's nicer than I am—a real charmer. Haven't seen her in three years, but she's supposed to graduate in six months, and I'll try to be there. If you're around then, I'll introduce you . . . no, maybe that wouldn't be smart. . . ."

The gray eyes were puzzled. "What do you mean?"

"I've seen the effect those damned ears have on the average female's hormones—and illogical as it is, *all* fathers tend to be over-protective."

The younger man was taken aback, then relaxed as the Doctor's grin broadened. "Oh . . ." he said, sheepishly. "You're joking with me. . . ."

Without warning, an alarm shrieked. Zar jumped. Lieutenant Uhura's voice could be heard throughout the ship. "Red alert. All stations, go to red alert. Battle stations, red alert." The siren continued to whoop.

McCoy stood up and his face hardened. "Here we go. At least the waiting is over."

Chapter XI

"All stations report red alert status, Captain," Uhura said.

"Entering sector 90.4, sir," Sulu's voice was calm.

"Decrease to sublight, helm, Lieutenant Uhura, are you picking up anything?"

"Yes, sir. We're being hailed by the *Lexington.*"

"Put it on audio, Lieutenant."

"Aye, sir."

A stutter of static, then a harried voice filled the bridge. Uhura made a hasty adjustment. ". . . lost our aft deflectors. Enemy vessels closing. *Enterprise,* are you there? Come in, *Enterprise.*"

"Open a channel, Lieutenant. Scramble it."

"Aye, sir. . . . Go ahead, sir."

Kirk kept his eyes fixed on the forward viewing screen as he spoke. "This is Captain Kirk of the *Enterprise* here, we are receiving you, *Lexington.* What is your status? Over."

A new voice. "Jim? This is Bob Wesley. We've held them off until now, but our aft deflectors are gone, and our port shield won't take another direct hit. Over."

"Hold on, Bob. . . . I've got you on my screens."

One large star and three smaller ones materialized and grew rapidly until the bridge crew could see the wounded vessel. The smaller Romulan ships circled her cautiously, wary of her greater firepower. Every time an opening presented itself, one of them would take advantage of their faster maneuverability to dart in, fire, and pull back out before the *Lexington* could bring her weaponry to bear.

"Ready forward phaser banks, Mr. Sulu."

"Phaser banks ready, sir."

"Fire a ten-second blast amidships on my order, then change course immediately to four-five-two, point zero, mark."

"Course four-five-two, point zero, mark, as soon as we've fired, aye sir. Phasers standing by."

Kirk scanned the instrument panel, counted seconds, then said quietly, "Fire." The deadly beams shot out, impaling the central Romulan warship directly. A sudden, blinding explosion flooded the viewscreen, then was gone as the *Enterprise* changed course. As the crew waited tensely, there came a shudder, then a slight lurch.

"A hit on the starboard deflectors, Captain, but not serious," Sulu reported.

"Change course to five-three-eight, mark two-four, Mr. Sulu. Let's go after the others."

"Aye, sir. . . . The *Lexington* just fired her main banks, sir."

Kirk was already watching the instruments, between glances at the viewing screen. The hit was a glancing one, and the Romulan was able to turn away, though she appeared to have limited maneuverability.

"That scorched her tailfeathers some. . . ." Commodore Wesley's voice came over the channel.

Kirk raised his voice, "Bob, I don't see the other one. Do you scan?"

"She used her cloaking device about a second after we fired."

"Prepare to pursue the one that was crippled, Mr. Sulu. Course three-two-six, mark zero-four."

"Aye, sir. Three-two-six, mark zero-four. . . . Captain, she just faded off the screen."

Kirk turned to his Science Officer. "Spock, switch all your sensors to infrared. We should be able to pick them up by their heat emissions, even if we can't see them or scan them."

The Vulcan bent over his sensors, and straightened after tense moments. "Negative, Captain. I picked up a faint trail, but they changed course often enough to mask it. This sector is full of radiation distortions that make scanning unreliable."

"Very well. Let's get back to the *Lexington.*"

As soon as Kirk assured himself that conditions aboard the other Federation vessel were stable, and repairs were already underway, he ordered the *Enterprise* back to yellow alert status. As the atmosphere on the bridge relaxed noticeably, the Captain beckoned his First Officer over. When the Vulcan was standing beside him, he asked quietly, "Your opinion, Spock?"

"A feint, sir. A diversionary tactic to accomplish something quite different than an attack on one of our starships. Otherwise, the *Lexington* should have been damaged far worse than she is. Romulans may be many things, but they are not cowards. They should not have run, even though we had them outclassed. Their warrior ethic would demand blood for blood."

"I agree. Now we have to figure out why they were prepared to either sacrifice themselves, or go against their own indoctrination in order to keep us busy. . . . The *first* thing I'm going to do, however, is get those archeologists off Gateway."

"A logical move, Captain. It has just occurred to me that before we arrived, the Romulans may have launched a shuttle. The *Lexington* might not have noticed it, since she was under attack from all sides. If they did launch one, I should be able to pick up life-form readings. . . ."

"Get on it." The Vulcan turned away, and Kirk addressed his Chief Communications Officer. "Lieutenant Uhura, contact Doctor Vargas on the planet's surface."

"Aye, sir."

The senior archeologist's face filled the viewscreen after a short pause. The image wavered and rippled erratically. "Captain Kirk?"

"Yes, Doctor. We've requested additional support from Star Fleet. Meanwhile, I want you and your staff to prepare to beam aboard. There's a possibility that the Romulans may have other ships in the system. How soon can you be ready?"

"I'll send my people aboard within two hours. However, I insist on staying here."

"Out of the question, Doctor. It's too dangerous."

"Kirk, we have records and artifacts that are invaluable. They must be preserved, at all costs. I'm not prepared to take the chance that they—or anything else on this planet—will fall into enemy hands."

"I'll beam down a security squad to help you pack up the artifacts, and you can transmit the records. Then Gateway will be maintained by my security forces until it's safe for you to beam back down."

"No. It's too dangerous to allow unauthorized personnel access to . . . the ruins. They could . . . damage them."

A yammer of static, and the image blanked, then came back on. Kirk straightened. "Doctor Vargas, I will take full precautions to see that my security guards do no . . . damage. I assume all responsibility. I'll beam down a team immediately to assist you in your packing—they'll have instructions to see that every one of you is transported aboard the ship with the records. Do you understand?" His voice was hard.

"My communications equipment is malfunctioning, Captain . . . I couldn't hear you . . . I'll watch for your security team . . ." The image bobbed and dipped, then steadied. "When all the equipment is packed, I'll contact you so you can beam up my staff and your guards."

"And *you,* Doctor. That's an order."

"I'm sorry, Captain. I can't hear you . . . my transmission is fading . . ."

Uhura turned away from her panel, as the image on the screen faded out. "She cut power, sir."

Kirk resisted the urge to slam his fist against the arm of the command chair. "The hell she couldn't hear me—I can't allow her to—" he controlled himself with an effort. "Uhura, was her equipment really malfunctioning?"

"Yes, sir. But she didn't lose the transmission—she cut it off."

"That's what I figured. Of all the stubborn—" He shook his head wearily. "I'd feel the same way, I guess. Still, I can't allow—"

Spock moved over to stand beside him, dropped his voice. "Captain, I must speak with you."

They faced each other in the deserted briefing room. The Vulcan lowered his lanky frame into a chair, stared at his hands for a moment. "Captain, when I worked on the equipment at the archeologists' camp, I realized it was badly in need of a complete overhaul. Their entire communications system is unreliable, and it is dangerous to depend on belt communicators. The time emanations from the Guardian, and the radiation pockets from the black stars in this sector make both communications and sensor readings subject to distortion. I recommend that, in the absence of reliable life-form readings, we evacuate the archeologists and post a security team—to be commanded by me. It may also be possible for me to rig a force field around the Guardian, which will provide additional protection."

Kirk nodded. "I agree with you on all points—except one. I'm not sending you down to Gateway with the security team. I need you here, to monitor the Guardian's emanations. With unreliable communications, I can't afford to take the chance of stranding you. Your knowledge of the Guardian is too valuable to risk."

"Yes, sir."

"Keep working on that idea of a force field as a

final protection for the time portal. Let's hope it doesn't come to that, though."

With the red alert over, Zar went back to the quad he shared with Steinberg and Cordova. He found them checking the charges in their phasers and clipping communicators to their belts. They were dressed in heavy-duty uniforms.

"Glad you came back, old man," Steinberg said, holding out a hand. "Juan and I wanted to say goodbye before we left."

Puzzled, Zar shook hands with both of them. "Where are you going, Dave?"

"Planetside. And a more barren, nasty ball of rock I've never seen. Not even any gorgeous women. Just a bunch of elderly archeologists to nursemaid. Oh well, orders is orders."

"Archeologists?"

"Yeah, some Doctor named Vargas is running the place. They're being evacuated, and we're going to stand guard over some old ruins. Why the Romulans could possibly want to invade *this* sector is beyond me . . . nothing but some burned-out suns, and an even more burned-out planet."

Juan Cordova grinned. "Just keep the old homestead clean while we're gone. When we get back, I'll give you the next lesson in 'Cordova's Course in Corruption.' Maybe booze and gambling didn't work out so well, but wait till next time! *Women.* . . ." Cordova jabbed Steinberg in the ribs with his elbow. "Look at that, Dave, he's blushing!"

Zar glared in mingled annoyance and amusement. "Juan, I've been looking for someone to practice that shoulder pinch on. Seems to me I just heard somebody volunteer . . ." He moved purposefully toward Cordova, who ducked behind Steinberg, laughing.

"Come on, Dave. We'd better get out of here before he really gets sore. . . ." The two security men picked up their kits and headed for the door. From the corridor, Cordova gave Zar a thumbs-up sign.

112

"See you later—stay away from strange men and dogs!"

One black eyebrow climbed. "Dogs? There aren't any dogs aboard the *Enterprise* . . ."

Steinberg shook his head. "He meant, 'take care of yourself.' We'll drop you a postcard from gorgeous Gateway. . . ."

"Dave, Juan!" Conscious of a strange reluctance to let them out of sight, Zar headed for the corridor and shouted after them, "What's a postcard?"

"We'll tell you when we get back—" The turbolift doors closed on them.

Suddenly the quad seemed much larger, and the silence was oppressive. Zar wandered into his cubicle, picked up his sketchbook, but couldn't concentrate on drawing. He realized that he was doodling, idle lines that formed—that formed a face. He stared, arrested by the familiar features in the rough sketch. Wiry hair, wrinkles, laugh lines . . . Doctor Vargas. . . .

He flung the sketchbook down, paced uneasily around the tiny room, then picked up the tape on Sarpeidon's history—the one that showed his cave paintings—and fed it into the viewer. He turned pages, scanning the words and illustrations absently, mentally replaying the conversation with Dave. Suddenly the lean fingers closed convulsively on the speed-control button, and Zar stared fixedly at the picture on the screen. *It can't be* . . . his gaze traveled involuntarily to the painting on the easel, and he flicked the viewer's "off" button with an uneasy frown.

Two mysteries. . . . The security man's words echoed in his mind again, and against his will the logical approach Spock had taught him set up the situation as an equation—and he didn't like the obvious solution. Finally, he went to the library computer console and keyed in a question. It clicked for a moment, then a light flickered on the console's screen. "No information in that area."

Unable to relax, he prowled the corridors of the ship. The *Enterprise* seemed oppressive, her corridors nearly deserted. Several times he turned suddenly, thinking someone was behind him, only to find himself alone. There was a sensation at the back of his neck that he recognized. He'd felt that prickling before, tracking prey, only to find that he, in turn, was being stalked.

He resisted the urge to drop in on McCoy, knowing the Doctor was busy. Briefly he considered going to the mess for a snack, but realized the churning in his stomach had nothing to do with real hunger. Blaming his increasing discomfort on loneliness, he attempted to dismiss it. After all, loneliness was something he'd learned to live with long ago; something that was always there, like the sun and the rocks and hunger. Funny now, but he'd thought in those days that *people* were the cure—people to be with, talk to . . . Instead, they only seemed to compound the problem. Not logical, but nevertheless true.

His thoughts turned to Spock, and he wondered what the Vulcan was doing, remembered the scene in the mess hall. Anger was gone, leaving only the futility—and shame. How naive he'd been! Something tightened in his abdomen, and he shivered, feeling queasy.

Unconsciously, his steps had taken him to the gym. It was deserted—few crew members off-duty because of the alert. He pulled off his shirt, bent to remove his boots. A workout would relax him.

Calisthenics, then a half-hour running on the treadmill, followed by a session with the weights. Hard physical activity was a known thing, thus comforting. Before, his life had depended on his strength, his reflexes, his stamina. Zar regarded his body as an instrument of survival, and took a dispassionate pleasure in its abilities.

He was handstanding on the rings, suspended nearly three meters above the deck, when he realized he had an audience. A young woman, wearing shorts

114

and gym shirt, stood looking up at him. Her frank, green-eyed gaze, even viewed from upside down, disconcerted him. His formerly smooth, economical movement became abrupt, awkward, and he nearly fell, managing at the last moment to get his feet under him, landing with an undignified thump.

"Are you all right?" she asked him.

He nodded, unable to think of anything to say.

Since coming aboard the *Enterprise,* he'd had little contact with any women except Lieutenant Uhura and Nurse Chapel. Uhura was his friend—as much as Scotty or Sulu. His relationship with Chapel was different—enigmatic. From her he sensed feelings he dimly remembered from Zarabeth, especially since the day Christine performed a chromosome analysis on him, afterward cautioning him to say nothing about it. His questions on the whys and wherefores proved futile. Chapel refused to discuss the subject.

His visitor hesitated, then smiled. "Didn't mean to startle you. I've been waiting for a chance to talk." Her voice was clear, pleasant. "I'm Teresa Mc-Nair."

"How do you do?" The formal words sounded inane, but they were the only ones he could think of. He was acutely conscious that she was young, and her head barely topped his shoulder. He "reached out" hesitantly, touched her emotions, and encountered expectation, mixed with a measuring appraisal of himself. *For some reason, she expected me to recognize her name. . . . Why?* "Why did you want to talk to me?" he asked.

"I feel a kind of proprietary interest, you might say." She saw his look of bafflement, and continued, "My secondary field is alien anthropology." Still that sense of some secret knowledge she expected him to respond to. . . .

"What's your primary field?" He was interested.

She lifted a quizzical eyebrow. "On duty, or off?"

"I beg your pardon?"

Her amusement lapped out in a wave, warming

him, although he didn't understand the reason for it. "You sound just like him. Never mind. I'm the most junior electronics tech on Chief Engineer Scott's staff. That means I get all the dirty work, and none of the glory." She cocked her head, studying his face, and suddenly he was aware of his sweat-damp hair, his bare feet. "It's hard to believe," she mused, almost to herself. "You're quite an artist, you know."

Pleased by the compliment, Zar nearly forgot himself and smiled openly at her. He repressed the grin just in time. "You've seen my paintings?"

"Oh, yes." Her smile faded, slowly, and then the green eyes lost their expectant air. "You don't have the slightest idea of what I've been talking about, do you?"

"No."

"I'm ashamed of myself—baiting you was an unworthy impulse. Don't worry, I'll never let on." She cocked her head, smiling differently this time. "Let's forget it. Would you . . . what's wrong?" He had put a hand to his head, and his eyes narrowed.

"I don't know . . . my head hurt." He shook himself, and the lines of pain faded. "It's better, now."

"You looked terrible for a second. You'd better check with Doctor McCoy."

"Maybe I will, later. Right now, I have to clean up."

"But I interrupted you. Go ahead with what you were doing."

"No, I was finished." He tried to think of some way to prolong the conversation, but his imagination failed him. He realized that he was simply standing there, looking at her, and abruptly turned away.

McNair stood where she was, watching the tall, slender figure. He had nearly reached the entrance when he staggered, then fell.

Pain! It slammed him behind his eyes, and he doubled over, retching. Dimly, Zar felt his shoulder slide across the doorframe, felt his knees buckling, and the coolness of the metal wall on his half-bare body.

blackness swirling with red boiled up, dimming his vision, and then there was nothing. . . .

By the time she reached him, McNair was sure he was dying. Every muscle contracted, head thrown back, he was gasping, huge, hurting lungfuls of air. The wheezing rasp of those breaths was painful to hear. As she dropped to her knees, avoiding the outflung arms, the gasps stopped. Knowing it was hopeless, she took his face between her hands, ready to pull him away from the bulkhead so she could get a clear airway and begin artificial resuscitation.

Suddenly, quite naturally, he began breathing again. McNair's mouth dropped open in genuine astonishment, and she sat back on her heels, fingers checking his wrist for a pulse. *Extremely fast . . . but maybe that's normal for him. Skin temperature hot, but that could be normal, also. He's sweating . . . but the exercise could account for that. . . .* Baffled, she shook her head.

Black lashes lifted, and he looked at her, then seemed to realize he was sprawled, half-prone against the wall. "What?" He tried to get up. McNair put a hand on his chest, emphatically.

"Don't. You'd better stay still."

"What happened?"

"You passed out. I never saw anything like it. I thought you were a goner. I'd have sworn you were gonal." At his look, she explained, "When people or animals die—especially violently—they spasm and breathe the way you were, just now."

"You're sure?"

"I lived through a Romulan assault when I was twelve. Most of the other colonists didn't. I'm sure."

He moved cautiously, not attempting to get up. The pain was only a memory now, gone as though it had never been. He felt slightly tired, and very hungry.

"How do you feel?" She was watching him closely.

"Fine." He didn't meet her eyes. Suddenly he was

117

conscious of the pressure of her hand, and the coo[l]
pleasurable sensation of her fingers on his ski[n.]
Through the contact, he felt her concern for hi[m]
and something else . . . dimly, in the background [of]
her mind, she was enjoying touching him. The re[-]
alization confused and elated him. He wanted to sta[y]
there, not moving, content to wait for—what? Th[e]
thought shook him, and before he realized what h[e]
was doing, he rolled over and got to his feet, lookin[g]
down at her. "I'm fine now."

McNair shook her head. "You sure didn't look fin[e]
a minute ago, but if you say so . . ." She put out [a]
hand to steady herself as she got her feet under he[r,]
and felt him catch it, pull her up with a strength tha[t]
surprised her until she remembered his ancestry, an[d]
the fact that Sarpeidon was a higher than Earth-ge[n]
planet.

"Has that ever happened to you before? Blackout[s]
or unconsciousness?"

"No . . ." He was hesitant, finally shook his hea[d.]
"No. I don't know what caused it . . . I don't re[-]
member . . ." He looked at her, and she dropped he[r]
eyes. He sensed that she was trying to keep some[-]
thing from him.

"What are you thinking of?"

"Nothing. You better see McCoy as soon as pos[-]
sible. Ask him about it."

The gray eyes were intent, and the inhuman cal[m]
of his face was a mask. "You're thinking about brai[n]
damage, aren't you? Epilepsy—things like that . .[.]
right?"

Reluctantly, she nodded.

"I suppose it's possible." She watched him repres[s]
a shiver. "There's something . . ." He shook hi[s]
head. "I can't remember."

After he showered, they went up to the mess roo[m]
to eat, and she told him about her home planet, an[d]
her training at Star Fleet Academy. He listened in[-]
tently, absorbed. McNair finished her account with [a]
description of the survival test each cadet had t[o]

ndergo during senior year. "It's brutal. They pick
ome godforsaken planet that's barely habitable, and
they dump you there bareass, no food, no weapons,
nd they expect you to *survive*."

He raised an eyebrow. "So?"

She glared at him for a moment, then realized he
asn't being smug. "So I survived," she said. "I
ad one narrow squeak, in the month I was there.
ell off a ledge and twisted my ankle—but I was
ucky, I could've broken my neck . . . what's
rong?"

He stared at her, horror darkening his eyes. "I
emember, now." She could barely hear him. "Seven
ears . . . I'd forgotten what death feels like. I've
ot to see the Captain."

Before Teresa McNair could voice any of the ques-
ons in her mind, he was gone.

Spock straightened up from his sensors, frowning
ightly. He jiggled a switch, punched buttons, re-
alibrated for possible—though unlikely—atmo-
pheric disturbance. The reading didn't change. He
icked the intercom switch. In a moment, the Cap-
ain's voice responded, a little fuzzily, "Kirk here."

"My apologies for waking you, Captain, but there
something on my sensors you should see."

"On my way," came the now wide-awake re-
ponse.

The Captain reached the bridge, found Spock sit-
ng in the command chair, chin on hand.

"What's going on?"

"I have been monitoring the planet's surface, and
e emanations from the ruins."

"There's been a change of some kind?"

For answer, the First Officer moved to the sensors,
nd pressed buttons. He lowered his voice. "When
first began monitoring, the surface readings showed
is." A set of figures flashed onto the screen. Spock
ressed another button. "Then, exactly six point four
inutes ago, the readings dropped, and have re-

119

mained constant again, but on a slightly lower level. He showed another set of figures.

"As though the emanations from the Guardian have been slightly . . . damped . . ." Kirk murmured studying the figures.

"Exactly."

"What could cause that effect?"

"A number of things. It could be the result of natural change in the time emanations from the ruin Or, it could be the result of a containing energy fie of some kind."

"Force field?" Kirk wondered.

"Possible. However, I should be able to pick u the presence of a force field, and my sensors sho nothing. In fact, there is a curious lack of positiv readings from the entire area of the Guardian."

"What about life-form readings—the landin party?"

"I recalibrated for the time disturbances . . . haven't been monitoring the landing party."

The Captain swung around. "Lieutenant Uhur what's the latest from the landing party?"

"They reported that the communications system o the planet was out of commission completely and th they would be using belt communicators. That wa almost two and a half hours ago. About an hour ag they signaled that they were beaming up the colle tion of artifacts, which they did. They're due to che back in again momentarily, sir." She broke off, fi gers dancing across her board. "There's somethin coming in now, Captain."

Kirk and Spock moved to stand beside her, as sh listened intently. Finally, she looked up at them, da eyes serious. "Captain, it's a message from Admir Komack. Star Base One has just reported that te Romulan vessels breached the Neutral Zone, headin in the direction of this sector. Their ETA is fourtee hours. He's dispatched five starships and a dread nought—at maximum warp, they should arrive i fourteen and a half hours. Maybe less."

"Thank you, Lieutenant. Contact the landing party. Tell them to stand by to beam up. Inform Lieutenant Harris that if Doctor Vargas gives him any problems, he has my permission to bring her forcibly. I can't have anyone left on that surface."

"Aye, sir." She turned back to her communications console.

"Spock, keep monitoring those emanations. Let me know if there's any further change in those readings." The Captain lowered his voice. "If there's even a chance that Romulans might reach the Guardian, we've got to prevent it. Even if that means destroying Gateway."

The Vulcan raised an eyebrow. "Captain, the scientific loss would be—"

"Irreparable. I know. But I may have no choice." Kirk turned back to the communications console. "Lieutenant, do you have that channel to the landing party yet?"

Uhura shook her head, adjusted the receptor in her ear, tried again. And again. Finally she looked back at Kirk, who was watching her tensely. "I'm sorry, sir. They don't answer. None of them answer."

Chapter XII

Over Spock's protests, Kirk led the rescue party himself. When they arrived at the coordinates of the first landing party, they found the area deserted. The rescue party huddled together, feeling the bite of the wind, while McCoy scanned the surroundings.

"No life-form readings—wait—very faint. This way." They began to run.

What was left of the landing party, as well as the archeologists, was strewn outside the wrecked camp building. Kirk clamped his teeth on his lip, and closed his eyes. A moment later, in control again, he joined McCoy, who was stooped over a prone figure.

Doctor Vargas was hardly recognizable. As the Captain approached, McCoy caught his eye and shook his head quickly.

"Can she talk, Bones?"

"I doubt it."

At the sound of their voices, the battered form stirred and opened its eyes. "Kirk . . ." The voice was so faint that the Captain shoved McCoy out of the way and nearly laid his ear on her mouth. He realized that she couldn't see him, and took her hand.

"I'm here, Doctor Vargas . . . who was it?"

". . . Rom . . ."

"Can you give her anything to help her talk, Bones?"

McCoy shook his head grimly. "No, Jim. Any stimulants will hasten the end."

"I didn't ask you that! Can you give her anything so she can talk?"

"Cordrazine, or trimethylphenidate, but—"

"Dammit, Bones, give 'em to her! I've *got* to know if the Romulans found the Guardian!"

McCoy mumbled under his breath, but got out his hypo, and Kirk heard it hiss as he held it against her arm. She opened her eyes, moaned.

"Did they find out the truth, Doctor Vargas?" He shook her slightly. "Do they know the location of the Guardian?"

"No . . . they had no drugs . . . crude methods . . . Torquemada . . . we fought . . . too many, too . . . strong. But we didn't . . . tell. Stop them. . . ." Her eyes closed, then opened wide, and she lurched under Kirk's hands. He heard her ragged gasps, then her voice again, astonishingly clear. "You must stop them. My Guardian . . . must not be used for . . ." The blue eyes closed again, then opened as her head lolled back. The Captain lowered her gently to the ground, as McCoy closed the eyes.

The rescue team was standing behind him when Kirk stood up. Masters, the Chief of Security, spoke up. "We checked, sir. No survivors. Butchers . . . seven of my people . . ." He swallowed, then spoke in a more normal tone. "Burial detail, Captain?"

"For sixteen? Ground's too hard. Have stretchers and body bags beamed down. Communications on scramble—tight beam. We don't want to be monitored. We'll have a group service when . . . when this is all over. Did they all die the same way?"

"Tortured? Yes. Why, Captain?"

Kirk clenched his fists, took a deep breath. "For information they couldn't have given, because they didn't have it. The archeologists are the real heroes. They died rather than tell. Have you searched the building?"

"Yes, sir. Ransacked. It's a good thing they got their records out."

"Yes, it is. I only wish we'd gotten the people out, too. Have you taken care of identification, or does McCoy need to get retinal patterns?"

"I took care of it, sir."

"Very well. Get that equipment down here on the double. If we stick around much longer, we may join them."

"Aye, sir."

Kirk beckoned to McCoy. "Let's check the Guardian. Set your phaser to kill."

The two walked amid the tumbled ruins until the camp building was behind them. The Captain halted, scanned the area, then took a small pair of distance lenses, scanned it again. He shook his head. "Bones, check our location on your tricorder."

The Doctor rattled off a string of coordinates. Kirk frowned. "I don't understand . . . we should be able to see it from here. Yet the landscape ahead is . . ." His voice changed. "Bones, it's *not there*. Where . . . do you suppose they've managed to *move* it somehow?"

"Hell, no, Jim. They couldn't move that thing. It must weigh tons. Besides, I'll bet it wouldn't operate in a different location. Where could it be, though?"

The Captain took out his communicator, adjusted the instrument to scramble. "Kirk to *Enterprise.*"

"*Enterprise,* Spock here."

"Have you been advised as to status here?"

"Affirmative, Captain."

"Are you still monitoring the readings from the ruins?"

"Yes, Captain. They've remained steady, at the level you saw them."

"Very well. Kirk out."

The Captain took another long look at the area, eyes puzzled. Ruins, fallen columns, blue-gray boulders, ashy sand . . . and that was all. "It can't just have vanished, Bones! It *must* be out there, some—" He broke off and turned to the Doctor. "That's it! It *is* out there, just where it should be— we just can't see it!" McCoy stared at him. Kirk nodded excitedly. "A new kind of cloaking device. They're projecting some sort of camouflage image at

124

us. The Guardian is about a hundred meters in front of us, but hidden by this . . . planetary cloaking device."

"You could be right, Jim. Sounds reasonable to me. If you are, though, how in hell are you going to keep the Romulans from using the Guardian—if we can't find it ourselves?"

"Can you scan it on your tricorder? Pick up any life-form readings that would tell us where they're located in there?"

The Medical Officer's tricorder hummed, then he shook his head disgustedly. "The time energies show up, but that's all. No way to pinpoint anything else. We're blind instrumentally, as well as visually."

Kirk looked thoughtful. "That gives me the beginnings of an idea . . . let's go back."

The first thing McCoy and Kirk saw when they materialized in the transporter room was Zar. The pallor of his face made his eyes look nearly black. His voice shook. "The landing party . . . they're all dead, aren't they? If only I had known earlier, they might still be alive . . . Juan and Dave . . . Doctor Vargas . . ."

McCoy stared, realized the younger man was in shock. Kirk moved, grabbed one rigid arm, shook it. The Captain's voice had the crack of an order. "Bones. Help me get him to sickbay."

Zar moved like an automaton as they propelled him into sickbay and pushed him into a seat. The Doctor worriedly took his pulse, glanced at Kirk. "Snap out of it, son. How'd you know about the landing party?"

The gray eyes blinked, lost some of their glazed look. "I . . . knew. The same way I knew . . . before. My head hurt, and I felt sick when I realized why the Romulans were attacking. The pain got worse—I passed out—and then it stopped. When I remembered the only time it had ever happened before, I knew that they were all dead." He slumped in his seat. "All dead . . . I might have been able to save them, if I hadn't . . ."

Kirk handed him a cup of black coffee, watched narrowly as the shaking fingers took it, then steadied the cup as it sloshed. "Take it easy, Zar. What do you mean, you know why the Romulans attacked?"

"It was obvious. They invaded this system to find the Guardian. It's potentially a deadly weapon. When I asked the computer about this sector, it didn't even know the time portal existed, so it *must* be classified. I wonder how the Romulans found out?"

"I don't know." Kirk shrugged, then pulled McCoy to one side as they watched Zar lean his head in his hands, exhausted. "What do you think, Bones?"

"I don't know, Jim. Precognition? Clairvoyance? Empathy with his friends' terror? I can't make guesses without more data."

The Captain's mouth tightened. "You're starting to sound like his father. I've got to get back to the bridge. Meanwhile, find out everything you can about this. It could be useful."

After Kirk left, McCoy gave his patient another cup of coffee. "Feeling better?"

"Yes." Zar shook his head. "I can hardly believe it, though. I talked to them only a few hours ago . . . then, to see them like that . . ." He pushed the cup away.

"But you weren't there. You couldn't see—" McCoy stopped.

"Yes, I did. In your mind, when you touched me."

"I'm sorry." McCoy scanned the features in front of him, realized that they were leaner, more drawn than they'd been seven weeks ago. The new maturity made him look less human, more like—"Zar, when did you start having these feelings of being sick?"

"Almost as soon as I said good-bye to Juan and Dave. Then I started drawing, and I drew Doctor Vargas. I tried to forget it, but it kept coming back, getting stronger, and finally, I passed out from the pain. When I came to, I was fine. It was only later,

126

while I was talking to . . . someone, when I realized what the sickness meant. . . ."

"What time was it the worst?"

"About two and a half hours after the landing party beamed down."

When they died . . . McCoy thought, remembering his brief examination of the bodies.

"You say this happened to you once before? When?"

The younger man's face was haunted. "When . . . she died . . . seven years ago. I'd forgotten, almost—I guess I wanted to forget. That's why I didn't connect it . . . it never worked for me—the time the vitha almost killed me, I had no warning. But when she fell . . . I was hunting, nearly . . . it must have been eight kilometers away. I felt the warning—sick, my head hurt, my stomach—and I knew something was wrong. I started to run back . . . I was about halfway when the pain came, and I knew it had happened. It knocked me out. . . . When I got there, I was too late . . . she was already . . . she'd been dead for at least an hour. . . ."

McCoy shook his head, and could think of nothing to say. Zar sat for a while, expression remote, then turned back to the Doctor. "When I realized that I had felt the same way as when my mother died, I knew that something must've happened to my friends, and that there was nothing I could do." His hands clenched. "That's the worst thing. To know it's going to happen, and that there's no way to stop it. Also, how am *I* going to manage, if every time I care about somebody and they die, I . . . feel it, too?"

"The more versed you become in the Vulcan mind-control techniques, the better off you'll be, I suspect." McCoy said. "That's not much comfort at the moment, I know. Incidentally, if you get any more of these . . . feelings, let me and the Captain know."

"All right."

"Now you'd better get out of here, and get some

127

sleep. You look like you could use it, and I've got some unpleasant work ahead."

Zar nodded and left. McCoy got a gown and gloves out of supplies, and went into the pathology bay, mentally gritting his teeth.

"So we have a problem." The Captain paced a few steps at the head of the briefing room table. "We know that the Romulans have activated the planetary cloaking device so that it surrounds the Guardian. As long as that device is activated, we have no way of determining where the Romulans *are* inside the perimeter of the screen. Also, we have no idea of the numbers we're facing. If we beam down a detachment, attempt to penetrate the encampment, we may find ourselves in their laps as soon as we step through . . . facing much greater numbers. Spock has calculated the area of the cloaking device, and it's large enough to mask a force of considerable strength. Every moment that goes by, is another that the Romulans have to use the Guardian. Our instruments are no help, except to tell us the size of the field. Frankly, I'm surprised they haven't already used the time portal, but we're still here, so I must assume they haven't. Yes, Lieutenant?" His gaze fixed on Uhura.

"Captain, you're basing a lot of your thinking on the premise that the Romulans *know* what the Guardian is—its capabilities as a time portal." Uhura shook her head thoughtfully. "Perhaps we ought to examine that. There are—how many would you say? Maybe twenty persons in the entire Federation—including the five of us here—who know about the Guardian. *What makes you think the Romulans know about it?*"

A babble of voices filled the briefing room. Uhura raised a hand for quiet, got it and continued, "Romulan knowledge of the powers of the Guardian would imply a security leak of some kind. To Star Fleet's knowledge, there's been no such leak." The dark-skinned woman leaned forward, eyes intent. "I don't believe there's been a leak, either. I don't think the Romulans know what the Guardian is, at all. I think they learned that we were guarding this planet for some unknown purpose. The Romulans probably assume that the Federation is protecting some military secret that's hidden on Gateway. Something manmade, an installation of some kind. Why else would a full-time guard of a starship be assigned to a burned-out cinder like that?" Uhura paused again, then continued. "Think of what it was like when the original landing party beamed down to Gateway. . . . Mr. Spock located the Guardian with his tricorder—and his scanners, on the ship. Romulan technology, thank goodness, isn't as advanced scientifically as ours. Militarily, they're powerful, but they lack intellectual curiosity. And the time portal won't respond, unless they ask a question . . . I'll bet they're so busy searching for some kind of weapon, or spaceship, that they've ignored the ruins—including the time portal."

Silence for a beat. Spock nodded, fingers steepled. "An extremely logical line of reasoning, Lieutenant. I'm inclined to agree, since your theory alone fits all the available facts." The Vulcan looked grave. "However, we cannot bank on their remaining unaware of the Guardian for long. Sooner or later, they will discover it. And when they do . . ."

The Captain shook his head. "We must prevent that. Even if it means using the phasers aboard the *Enterprise* and the *Lexington* to wipe out the planet. We've got less than thirteen hours now, before the Romulan fleet arrives. Hopefully, our ships will be right on their tails, but we can't afford to chance it."

The expressions around the table were eloquent. Kirk's eyes were bleak. "I know that the loss to the Universe would be great—the scientific and historical knowledge could never be regained. There's another danger, also. The Guardian may very well have its own defense systems. Any attempt to destroy it might cause it to blow the lot of us—Romulans *and*

129

Humans—out of space. Even if it has no defenses of its own, its power source is so unthinkably great that its destruction might mean the end of this entire sector. Any way we look at it, the risks are great. And, if it's necessary to destroy the planet, I'll make that decision. That way, whatever the ramifications, I alone will be held responsible. I don't want to turn our phasers on the Guardian—but that may well be the only choice." He stood at the head of the table, then after a long second, straightened his shoulders. "Dismissed."

Chapter XIII

Captain's Log Stardate 7340.37

"We remain on yellow alert, awaiting the arrival of the Romulan fleet, and Federation reinforcements. Within the next twelve hours, I must either protect the time portal against unauthorized use, or destroy Gateway. The only possible solution I can think of involves breaking General Order Nine, but at this point, I have little choice. Kirk out."

The Captain punched the "record" button and slumped into his chair, casting a wistful look at his bunk. Instead, he keyed for another cup of coffee, and opened a channel on the intercom.

"Spock here."

"Have you spoken with Doctor McCoy about what happened in the transporter room when the landing party returned?"

"No, Captain."

"Zar was there. Somehow he knew, without being told, what had happened on the surface—that the landing party had been wiped out. Have you seen him since?"

"No."

"He was extremely shaken up by the whole thing. Apparently he was linked in some way to his friends, Cordova and Steinburg, and experienced their deaths. McCoy suggests precognition, or possibly clairvoyance. Any ideas?"

The Vulcan was slow in answering. "No, Captain. The qualities you have mentioned are not unknown among telepaths, but I have never had direct experience with either, except once . . ."

"I remember. The *Intrepid.* As I recall, it was painful."

"Yes. You saw him in the transporter room?"

"Yes. He said that the initial shock knocked him out, but by the time he saw us, he was mostly blaming himself because he hadn't warned us in time to save them. Seems that he'd been feeling uneasy for a couple of hours before their deaths."

"Is he in sickbay now?"

"No, that's why I contacted you. I can't locate him, and I want to ask him a few questions about this ability of his. Is it true that he can sense the presence of other life-forms by tuning in on their emotional output? He doesn't have to be in physical contact?"

"Yes, although the life-form must be reasonably high on the evolutionary scale. Lower life-forms, insects for example, experience little emotion that is translatable in sentient terms."

"That's what I thought. Good. Order Mr. Scott to relieve you, and come down to my quarters. Bring Zar with you. Kirk out."

The Vulcan depressed the intercom switch with a slight frown, one that deepened when there was no response from Zar's quad. He tried the gym, the library, the recreation areas. Nothing. Turning command over to the Chief Engineer, he headed for his own quarters, following what Kirk would have termed a hunch, and Spock thought of as logical deduction. . . .

The door opened, the familiarity of his cabin, bunk, chair, microreader, tapes, everything normal. . . . His eyes stopped their scan, focused on a still form lying on the floor of the alcove, half-hidden by the crimson drapery. . . .

For a split second he stood poised, unable to make

132

himself move, then his body took over, walking him without volition to that black-clad shape. As he bent down, fingers curved to grasp the shoulder gently, Zar stirred, grunted and woke.

The Vulcan's voice was harsh with relief. "What are you doing here?"

The younger man was obviously embarrassed. "I couldn't stay in the quad. It was so . . . empty. So I came here to return the tape on my planet's history, and I decided to view that tape on Vulcan art-forms. After a while I was tired. I didn't expect you back. Aren't you on duty?"

"Yes. Why didn't you use the bunk?"

The gray eyes widened. "It's your bunk, not mine. Besides, I can sleep anywhere."

One eyebrow flicked upward. "Obviously. Get up. The Captain wants to see you. Come on."

"Me?"

"Actually, both of us. I don't know why."

Kirk was starting on his second cup of black coffee, rubbing eyes that felt sand-blasted from fatigue, when the door signal flashed. "Come." he called, and waved his visitors to seats. "Sit down, please. I have a few questions, and a proposition for you." He sat back on his bunk, cradling his coffee, while two sets of eyes, one inquisitive, one reserved, regarded him steadily.

"Zar, can you tell if a sentient life-form is near you, without seeing it?"

The younger man nodded. "I can with every life-form I've encountered."

"Can you block your mind the way Spock can? For instance, screen out pain and prevent your mind from being read by drugs, and so forth?"

"I can block myself so that no telepath can read me against my will. Those other things . . . I don't know."

Spock raised an eyebrow. "He has a natural mind-shield of a high order. The pain block and resistance to drugs is a technique requiring a great deal of study

133

and discipline, as well as physiological controls he doesn't possess. Possibly, with a more qualified instructor, he could develop them. I'm not prepared to postulate."

"But his mind can't be read against his will by mindmelding?" Kirk leaned forward.

"No more than mine can." The Vulcan looked uneasy as he answered.

"What do we know about Romulan telepathic abilities?"

"Almost nothing, Captain. They exist, but in what degree it is impossible to speculate." Spock's eyes narrowed. "Captain, there is only one logical reason for your asking these questions . . . the answer is 'no.' "

Kirk frowned. "I didn't ask you, did I?"

Zar looked at the two officers, puzzled. "What are you talking about? Captain, what was your proposition?"

"Has Spock told you about the cloaking device the Romulans have set up around the Guardian's location?"

"No, he hasn't told me anything. Obviously, the Romulans haven't utilized the time portal, at least in a manner that's discernible to us . . . however, that raises an interesting question. Would we actually be aware of it, if history *did* change around us? It's possible we would simply adjust to the changes in the fabric of existence around us unknowingly . . . I wonder what equations for such a problem would look like . . ."

Spock looked interested. "A fascinating concept. Hypothetically, if the—"

The Captain raised his hand. "I hate to interrupt, but while you two sit there and discuss the logic involved, the time-continuum *may* change. Zar, the situation is this . . ." Kirk continued, outlining the problem, and concluded, ". . . so we have to penetrate this cloaking device, and somehow protect the time portal before the Romulans discover it. To do this, we must get inside the perimeter of the screen."

The younger man looked thoughtful. "You want me to get inside this cloaking device, because I can sense the presence of the Romulans, without seeing them . . . is that correct?"

"Can you do it?"

The gray eyes began to shine. "I'll try, sir. Once I get inside without getting caught, what will I do to the time portal?"

"That's where Spock comes in. He's figured out a way to rig a force field around the Guardian that will prevent the Romulans from going through, even if they do discover it. By the time they could break through the shield, we should have reinforcements here."

"Yes, sir." Zar stood up. "When do we go?"

" 'We' are not going." The Vulcan was also on his feet, and the flat statement rang like a challenge. "At least you're not. I am perfectly capable of installing that force field alone. Captain—" without turning his head, "surely you are aware that you are violating General Order Nine in requesting civilian assistance in this matter?"

"I'm doing the only thing I can to protect the Guardian short of destroying the entire planet. I'm willing to break General Order Nine to accomplish that."

"It's not your decision to make, Captain." Spock's eyes turned to Kirk's, and the expression in them made the Captain blink, before his own gaze hardened. The Vulcan's voice was harsh. "Zar, return to your quarters."

"No, sir." Something about the cold, quiet tone made both officers look at him. "You're right, it's not his decision to make—it's mine. I'm going."

"No." The Vulcan shook his head. "It's too dangerous. I cannot allow it. I will go alone."

"That's where you're wrong. *I* will go alone, if necessary. The Captain can get someone to set up the force field, but you can't find anyone else that can get you through that screen, and warn you of enemies once you're inside. It would be better if I went alone, as a matter of fact. Then I wouldn't have to worry about you slowing me down."

"That's enough of that." Kirk snapped. "You both go, or nobody goes, and I begin the destruction." Spock turned to look at him, and the Vulcan's eyes made the Captain clench his fists. "Spock, I know what you're thinking. *But I have no choice.* I'd sacrifice any person on this ship, starting with myself, to keep the Romulans from getting a chance at the time portal. It's my duty, and nobody, not even you, can interfere with that." He looked at Zar, and continued. "I'm sending Zar, because he's willing to go, and he has this unique . . . perception, whatever you call it, and therefore has the best chance of getting in, and getting back out, alive. And I'm asking you to go too, because you can protect him better than anyone else. If you prefer, I'll send Zar and somebody else. Think it over. We haven't much time."

Spock turned back to Zar, who was standing quietly, hands at his sides, open challenge in his eyes. The First Officer snapped out a sentence in a language Kirk assumed was Vulcan. The younger man's chin came up, and he answered with an equally sharp manner in the same language. Spock's mouth tightened, then he nodded, slowly, reluctantly.

Without another word, the young man left the room. The Captain turned to his First Officer. "Well, who won?"

"He's gone to get ready." Spock didn't meet his eyes. Kirk knew that the Vulcan was as angry as he'd ever seen him—at both of them.

"I wish there were some other way, Spock." The Captain sighed. "Well, at least it won't take long. In an hour—two at the outside—you'll be back aboard, and the Guardian will be safe." He paused. "It took courage to stand up to you the way he did."

"It was total disrespect."

136

"I don't think he meant it that way . . ." Kirk remembered the look on Spock's face when Zar had announced that he'd only slow him down. "He's cocky, though . . . I was like that, myself, at one time." He grinned reminiscently. "My old man had hell to pay trying to discipline me—nothing worked. Did your father ever have the same problem?"

The Vulcan raised an astonished eyebrow, saw Kirk's knowing grin and gave in. "Vulcan methods worked on me . . . usually."

"Well, if you want, when this is over, I'll order up a security squad, and we can take turns walloping him."

The Captain was waiting when the two volunteers, clad alike in dark, insulated coveralls, entered the transporter room. Watching them as they moved to strap on phasers and communicators, he was struck again by the similarities—and the differences. Both moved easily, gracefully, but Spock's grace was economical, precise, while Zar's was . . . feline? Kirk rejected the word, but could find no better one.

When they stood on the transporter pads, Spock holding the portable force-field unit, the Captain flicked switches, was rewarded by an answering hum. "Remember, you've got twelve hours to set up that unit and get back to the landing coordinates, before Bob and I start taking that planet apart. If you're still on it . . ."

"Understood, Captain." Spock nodded. A second later, the two figures shimmered into nothingness.

Gateway was quiet, except for the wind, and even that seemed strangely muted. The ever-present ruins closed in around them, as they picked their way cautiously over the boulders and chunks of fallen buildings. The ashy platinum sand, studded with silica-like sparkles, was too fine to hold their footprints. Within minutes, all traces of their passage were gone.

Spock checked his tricorder often, and finally sig-

137

naled a halt. "The screen should begin directly in front of us," he said in a low voice.

Zar looked, could see nothing but more rocks and tumbled structures ahead—a mirror image of what lay behind them, even though his sense of direction told him the Guardian was about forty meters in front of him. He narrowed his eyes, and sensed, more than saw, a shimmer in the air in front of him. "I can see it."

"Yes. Can you pick up anything on the other side of the screen?"

"Two—maybe three, near the Guardian. We'll have to angle in from the left."

Even though Zar's perception told him that the way ahead was clear, they dropped to hands and knees to cross the device's camouflage barrier a few minutes later. Both were conscious of a tingling sensation, but that passed as they moved away. Spock started to get to his feet, but Zar grabbed his arm. "Stay down—they're all around this area. Follow me."

The Vulcan found himself hard put to keep up, as they dodged from outcrop to outcrop, wiggling prone much of the time. They were well-camouflaged themselves, smeared with ashy dust, by the time they reached a point where they could see the time portal.

Beside the monolith, still quiescent, a small, alien craft stood, hatch open. Romulans were busy unloading it. They were paying no attention to the huge stone figure, but there was no way for anyone to get near the Guardian without being seen immediately.

Spock jerked his head in silent command, and they withdrew until they were a safe distance away. Zar located a rocky niche sheltered from sight and the wind, and they settled down to await the completion of the unloading. "We can only hope that the Romulans are as efficient at unloading a shuttlecraft as they are at everything else," Spock said. "We have eleven hours, twenty-four point three minutes before the Captain's deadline."

Zar nodded silently, and the two sat, listening to the wind, as the minutes limped by. The younger man used his perception to check on the Romulan's presence, occasionally scrambling up to peer out at the scene. Finally, to keep himself from getting sleepy, he turned to the silent figure beside him. "I was reading my biology lesson the other day . . ."

"Yes?"

"There was a discussion of hybrids . . . I'm one . . ."

"No. I am." Zar was startled. "You? I thought . . ." he trailed off in confusion.

"I'm half Human. Didn't you know? I thought McCoy would tell you. Why does the fact surprise you?"

"Most hybrids are sterile . . ." the young man blurted, wishing he could retrieve the remark as soon as it was voiced.

Immediately, he picked up a current of wry amusement, though Spock's voice was unchanged. "I'm not. Obviously."

"That means I'm only one-quarter Vulcan . . . I thought I was half. You don't show any signs of your Human ancestry."

"Thank you." The amusement deepened.

"Which of your parents is Vulcan?"

"My father, Sarek, former ambassador to Earth, and several other planets, including the seat of the Federation Council."

"Sarek of Vulcan? I've read about him . . . an extremely old and respected family."

"Yes. Not an easy kinship to uphold."

"Still, it must be a good feeling to know where you belong . . . no matter where you go, some world claims you, and you're part of it. A home. I miss that . . ." Zar stopped abruptly, swallowed to relieve the sudden tightness at the back of his throat, and had a vision of sharp, ice-covered peaks and plunging valleys. *And the picture I saw . . . what does it mean?* He glanced over at the Vulcan, found that he

139

was watching him closely, his face a blur in the shadow. The intent gaze was disconcerting, and Zar hastily scrambled over to look out at the landing craft. "They're still unloading. . . ."

Spock looked at him calmly. "I filed a statement for Vulcan citizenship for you with the leader of the Family, the day we returned from Sarpeidon. T'Pau knows about you. You should make your claim to her, if anything happens to me."

Zar found the implication disturbing, and his tone was sharper than he'd intended. "If anything happens to you, there's not much chance that I'll be alive, either. . . . How much time left?"

"Eleven hours, twelve point three minutes."

"I'm not sure I'd make that claim—even though it would be good to have a . . . home. Vulcan social traditions, according to what I've read, are somewhat rigid."

"I know. Family expectations can be difficult to integrate with personal ambitions . . . needs. The Family determines most life-choices—or tries to. Career . . . even marriage. You would be expected to preserve the succession . . . uphold the tradition."

"You mean marry to order?" The idea seemed very alien to the younger man, and he shuddered slightly. *There would be no joy in that, only duty.* Ironically, his mother's face, lips curved in a smile of remembrance spilled into his mind, warring with the picture that had been there since his talk with Kirk, and he wondered futilely what the truth was. *Don't think about it. Concentrate on something else.* "Marriage . . . that's not a subject I ever considered. As for the succession, I wonder if I could even interbreed with a full-blooded Vulcan . . . or Human, for that matter?"

"I don't know. Probably . . . you may not want to consider marriage to a Vulcan, however."

"Why?"

"Because of the pon farr."

"Pon farr? That translates to 'time of mating,' or 'time of wedding.' What is it?"

Spock drew a deep breath, and Zar could sense the emotions—embarrassment, reticence. Then he told him, his voice quiet, of the mating drive that occurred every seven years, and of the madness that could result . . . even to the point of death, if the urge was denied too long.

The younger man was stunned. "That's how Vulcans marry?" His next thought made his eyes widen. "That's not going to happen to *me,* is it?"

The First Officer was carefully examining a small, nondescript pebble. "Probably not," he said, without looking up. "It is largely brought about by racial conditioning. You could feel vestiges, but I doubt that you would experience the insanity."

"Insanity . . ." Zar shivered suddenly. "Have you ever . . . did you . . ."

"Once."

Zar gritted his teeth to stop the next question, but it rushed out anyway, as though it had a life of its own. "Was that with . . ." He swallowed, "I mean, when . . ."

"No." He had expected resentment from the Vulcan, but could detect none in the flat voice, sense none in the emotional output. "It happened on Vulcan, several years ago."

"Then you're married . . . I didn't know." Zar wondered fleetingly if he had brother or sisters. *Legitimate ones,* one part of his mind sneered. But Spock shook his head.

"No. My prospective consort chose the challenge. No marriage took place." The pebble dropped, stirring the ashy sand. "Are they still unloading the ship?"

The gray eyes narrowed, as Zar concentrated on the actions he could not see. "Yes—how much time left?"

"Eleven hours, five point five minutes." Spock retrieved the pebble, dropped it again, to look at his

141

companion squarely. "Do you have any more questions about . . . what we've been discussing? It is something you should know—though I never envisioned myself giving what McCoy might term a 'straight from the shoulder.' "

Zar understood neither the reference, nor the self-deprecation that accompanied it. Something else was bothering him. After a long silence, he ventured, "Only every seven *years?*"

Again he sensed amusement, this time betrayed in the Vulcan's voice. "You sound dismayed. Surely you know by now whether you're subject to that time constraint or not . . . even for those of us who are, it can be accelerated or retarded under certain circumstances. Sometimes circumvented entirely."

This time it was Zar's turn to voice a dry, "Obviously."

"Very few non-Vulcans even know that the pon farr exists. It is not a subject for light discussion. Most Vulcans prefer to forget about it . . . as much as possible."

"I understand." The wind tumbled through the ruins like the ghost of a long-dead surf. After a few minutes, the younger man peered out at the landing craft. "There are only two of them left, now. Do you want to try it?"

"We still have time. Wait a few more minutes. The fewer we have to deal with, the better our chances for remaining undetected."

Zar nodded, and settled back against the rock. "I've read about Sarek, but never any mention of his Human wife. Is she from Earth?"

"Yes. While he was ambassador to Earth, he married Amanda Grayson, a teacher."

"A teacher—that's funny."

"What do you mean?"

"Both of our mothers were teachers . . . I wonder if they're all alike?"

"Teachers, or mothers?" The Vulcan leaned back

142

against the rock, and looked up at the perpetually star-spattered sky.

"Both, I guess. In some ways she was a harder taskmaster than you are. We had no one but each other to talk to, but I couldn't make any grammatical mistakes without being corrected."

"That sounds like my mother, too—someday, I suppose you'll meet her." The thought carried amusement.

"You're amused. Why?"

"How can you tell that?"

"I can pick up your emotions. When we're in close proximity, and there aren't any Humans to drown them out. Humans are like listening to ordinary voices in a room, and sometimes they even shout. You're like a whisper in a large room . . . but I can hear a whisper, if there's nothing to distract my attention." Zar paused, then continued, "Your emotions are clear-cut, not jumbled, like Human ones. You feel one thing at a time—the way you think."

"Vulcans are not supposed to feel emotions at all." Spock said, his voice distant.

"I know. However, I'd be willing to bet that they all do. Don't worry, I can screen it out, if it bothers you. . . . You forgot to tell me what was funny."

"I was thinking of my mother. I suddenly envisioned her reaction if somebody told her that she had a twenty-six-year-old grandson. Considering Sarpeidon's year as it relates to Terran Standard, you're nearly twenty-eight, actually. Amanda would . . ." The Vulcan shook his head slightly, evidently picturing the reaction again.

Zar sensed the amusement, stronger than before. Curiosity gnawed at him, and he finally asked, "What *would* her reaction be?"

"Probably the same as mine was, considering that she isn't old enough to have a grandson your age."

"You thought that when you first found me . . . about yourself, and my age, I mean?"

"Yes." Spock noted the younger man's surprise,

and said, nettled, "It's true, after all. How old do you think I am?"

"I don't know. I never thought about it . . . fairly old, I guess."

"The situation is a physical impossibility."

"Oh."

Silence for several minutes. Then the Vulcan said, abruptly, "There's something I must tell you."

"What?"

"The meaning of the word 'krenath.' "

Zar had forgotten his mention of the word to Kirk. He felt his face grow hot, and was glad it was dark.

"On Earth, in the past, Humans illogically placed the blame for illegitimacy on the children of the union. Fortunately, the word 'bastard' now has no real literal meaning. Colloquially, it is used to denote a person who is undesirable, for various unspecified reasons." Spock took a deep breath, then continued, "On Vulcan, where family is one of the most important factors in a person's life, it is different. The krenath are regarded as wronged by the mistakes of their elders. They are accorded every possible redress, including full status in both families. It's the parents who are stigmatized."

The younger man thought for a long moment, felt his anger draining away. He realized something of the effort it had cost the Vulcan to voice that explanation.

"So you would be admitting to a serious breach of . . . custom . . . by acknowledging me?"

"Yes."

Zar fought back the question that came to his mind. It obviously *wasn't* the Vulcan's intention to acknowledge him—at least while Spock was still alive. Embarrassed, he scrambled over to peer out, then turned back excitedly. "They've gone. All except one guard. Let's move."

Chapter XIV

The bridge of the *Enterprise* was quiet, the atmosphere one of silent expectation. Kirk slumped in his command chair, sipping yet another cup of coffee—one that he hastily put down as he straightened to face Lieutenant Sulu. The young helmsman repressed a sigh—the waiting was wearing on all of them. "Subspace sweep completed, sir. No sign of any approaching craft."

"Very good, Mr. Sulu. Next sweep in ten minutes, then shorten the intervals by one minute each time."

"Aye, sir."

"Lieutenant Uhura, have you picked up anything from the approaching Federation craft giving a new ETA?"

"No, sir. I'll inform you immediately if I do." She sounded a bit huffy. The Captain realized he was telling her how to do her job, a vice he normally avoided. Nothing bred sloppiness and inefficiency in subordinates faster. He shook his head, realizing that fatigue was making inroads on his judgment and efficiency.

He heard the bridge door, then McCoy stood at his elbow. Kirk looked up, realized that the Doctor was upset. "What's up, Bones?"

"Jim, I've looked all over the ship for Zar, and can't find him. Nobody's seen him. Or Spock. Do you know where they are?"

"I sent them down to Gateway to rig a force field around the Guardian." The Captain's voice was low, even.

"You *what?*" The Doctor spoke in a whisper, but Sulu looked around, hastily turned back to the navigational controls.

"Mr. Sulu, you have the con. I'll be in the small briefing room with Doctor McCoy. Inform me immediately of any developments."

"Aye, sir."

In private, McCoy repeated his question, only several decibels louder. Kirk gave him a hard look, then snapped, "You're dangerously close to insubordination, Doctor. I suggest you sit down and shut up."

McCoy sat, and said quietly, "Sorry. It won't happen again."

The Captain sat down opposite him and smiled wearily. "No hard feelings, Bones. It's a rough time for all of us."

"Yeah, tell me about it. I just finished those autopsies."

"I sent Zar and Spock down to the surface, because Spock can rig that force field faster than anyone on this ship—with the possible exception of Scotty, whom I can't spare if there's a fight. And I sent Zar—or, rather, he volunteered to go, because he can use that power of his to warn them of Romulans."

McCoy gave him a long look. "Jim, you must realize that if the Romulans don't kill them, those two will probably do each other in. The situation there is explosive."

"I admit your point, but I had no choice. Just as I'll have no choice but to begin the destruction of Gateway in roughly ten and a half hours if they fail—whether or not they're back by then."

The Doctor stared. "You wouldn't do that, Jim. . . ."

"You know I will. But it won't be necessary. They should be back any time. I sent the two best-equipped people I could, and if they can't pull this off, nobody can."

"But . . . Zar . . . he has no training, no military

146

experience. The Romulans are ruthless. If they capture him, it'll be the landing party all over again."

"He's got more training and experience at sheer survival than any of us. He could beat any of us at rough-country scouting—you said so yourself, if I recall. And if the Romulans are savage, remember, Zar isn't so civilized by a long shot."

McCoy didn't look reassured. Kirk shook his head. "I did what I had to, Bones. Don't look like that . . . anybody would think *you're* his father. Not Spock."

The Doctor took a deep breath. "You're right, Jim. Sorry I got out of line. What I really came up to the bridge to talk to you about *was* you." He pointed at the Captain. "Have you looked at yourself lately? You look like Matt Decker, and you're starting to act like him. You need sleep. Now, are you going to crawl in the sack and let me give you a hypo to knock you out for four or five hours—six would be better—or am I going to have to declare you unfit for duty?"

Kirk sighed. "Blackmail again, Doctor?"

"Sorry, Jim. *I'm* doing what *I* have to. Besides, there's nothing you can do at the moment, is there?"

"You win, Bones." He keyed the intercom. "Mr. Sulu?"

"Yes, Captain?"

"I'm going to my quarters. Notify me immediately of any changes in patrol status, or if Mr. Spock reports in. He's on Gateway's surface. He should be requesting beam-up any time. Kirk out."

He stood up, waving the Doctor aside. "I'm going, Bones. And I don't need a hypo. I want to see that I'm called in five hours, if Sulu hasn't paged me before. Five hours . . . any more than that, and I'll court-martial you, understand?" He stifled a yawn, then rubbed his bloodshot hazel eyes fiercely.

"Yes, sir!" McCoy snapped to attention in his best pseudo-military manner. He did it poorly.

The Captain shook his head as he left. "It's a good

thing you didn't have to go through the Academy. . . ." The door to the briefing room closed behind him.

McCoy slumped back into his seat, leaning his head in his hands. Against his will, he thought of angry eyes, both black and gray, and powerful hands. . . .

He began to curse, very quietly.

Chapter XV

Spock and Zar worked their way over until they were about fifteen meters from the Romulan guard. He was standing with his back to them, beside the ship, wearing the uniform and ramrod stance of a Centurion. Every five minutes exactly, he'd pace the length of the craft, scanning the surroundings alertly.

The Vulcan's whisper was so low the younger man had to strain to hear him. "Go behind the ship and create a diversion—not too loud. I'll take care of the guard."

Zar snorted rudely, hissed, "That's highly illogical, and you know it. I'm the one who can get over there and take care of him quietly. No noise, no other Romulans. Wait here."

Spock made a grab for his ankles, but he was gone, melting into the shadows as though he'd never existed. The Vulcan strained his eyes and finally caught sight of him on the other side of the ship, hidden by the inky shadow of a boulder. Crouching low, he slid around the hull, and Spock saw something gleam in his hand.

The Centurion was halfway down the length of his beat when Zar leaped. The movement was so fast that it was all over before it registered in the First Officer's mind. Against his will, his brain slowed it down and replayed it.

The catlike leap—then grabbing the guard's chin, dragging his head back—the slash of knife across throat in one quick motion—and Zar stepped back quickly to avoid the blood.

149

It took Spock perhaps a half-minute to stand up and cover those fifteen meters. When he reached Zar the young man was sitting on his heels, wiping the blood off his knife onto one still-twitching shoulder. He looked up, eyes silver in the dim light.

Spock felt his insides heave. "What are you going to do now? Gut him and hang him?"

The feral light died slowly in the gray eyes. "What?"

"You took a life . . . there was no reason for it . . . no excuse."

Zar barely glanced at the blood-soaked figure, then shrugged. "He was an enemy. What does his life matter?"

Spock clenched his fists, then forced them open again. His words were measured, deliberate. "You have no right to consider yourself Vulcan, if you can do this."

The younger man hadn't missed the gesture, and his face hardened as he stood to face the other. His voice was cold. "I acted logically. Why let him live, and take a chance on his raising the alarm? Besides, he and his kind killed my friends . . . and not as mercifully. I killed quickly, They died for a long time."

Spock shook his head. "Their violence doesn't excuse yours. There was no reason to kill. . . . On Vulcan, life is precious . . . it can never be returned or replaced. If I had any idea that you intended . . . this . . . I would have stopped you." He began to turn away, hesitated. "Warn me immediately if anyone approaches." His glance at the Centurion held revulsion. "You'd better hide the body."

Zar ground his teeth together so hard his jaw muscles hurt, as he watched him walk away. Then, swallowing convulsively, he bent over, sheathed the knife and picked up the guard.

The Science Officer had been working for nearly an hour, when Zar, formerly a motionless shadow among shadows, suddenly moved toward him. Dropping down at the Vulcan's side, he whispered, "How much longer?"

"Approximately four minutes to finish these settings, then I can turn the power on."

The younger man shook his head. "Too much time. We've got to hide and get out of here. Somebody's coming. Now." The gray eyes narrowed as his expression turned inward, listening. "More than one."

Spock hesitated, then resumed working. "I'll set it, then hide. You get out of sight."

"I'm not leaving you. I may not be Vulcan . . . but I'm no coward." Again that far-away look. "We haven't got a chance. There are six of them. They'll be here any minute!"

The First Officer gritted his teeth, hesitated another long second, then stood up and kicked rocks over the unit. "We'll wait until they pass, then come back. Head for those ruins over there."

They ran. When they reached the ruins, a ghostly tumbled pile of blocks that might have been a collapsed building, or a highway, or almost anything else, they climbed quickly to the top. There was a large boulder overhanging the others, with a small hollow beneath. They just fit.

The two men could see the Romulans through a narrow slit in the bottom of the boulder that gave them limited vision. The six soldiers milled in confusion, obviously searching for the vanished guard. Then they moved away, and the two in hiding were dependent on Zar's ability to tap into the searchers' emotions. They crouched, not talking, except when the young man breathed a comment.

"They're puzzled."

Two minutes went by.

"Suspicion . . . they've called for help. . . ."

Another ten minutes.

"More of them. All looking."

An hour and a half.

"Surprise. Shock, Anger. One found him."

Now they could see the enemy crossing and re-crossing their vision slit in pairs. Once they crouched, hands and faces hidden, grateful for their dark clothing when a Romulan crawled up and glanced casually down into their hiding place. The overhang was dark; he didn't see them.

Six and a half hours. They didn't speak, only watched with increasing tension as the searchers combed the ruins with the ruthless patience of experienced hunters. Zar was familiar enough with that kind of patience to know that the Romulans would keep looking until they were sure the intruders were gone. In these ruins, that could take a very long time indeed.

Gradually, as time crept by for the two men cramped into the tiny hiding place, the number of Romulans searching dwindled. Finally, when fifteen minutes had passed without sight of one, and Zar reported that he could sense none in the immediate area, they crawled out of the rocks, straightening knotted muscles in relief. "How much time left?" Zar asked, dreading the answer.

"Thirty-four point two minutes until the Captain begins the destruction pattern. Depending on where he implements it first, we may have some additional time, until the planet begins breaking up. I would not count on it, however."

"We can't hurry, though. I can pick them up all over the place. . . . Stay low, and follow me. I'll keep to cover when I can."

They headed to the left, a slow scouting sneak toward the perimeter of the cloaking device screen. By mutual unspoken agreement, they knew that any further attempt to return to the Guardian would be suicidal.

Crouch and run a few meters, dodge behind a fallen column or boulder, scan the area ahead, crouch, drop to hands and knees or belly to worm across an open space—and then do it over again. . . .

Both men were tough, strong, but soon the pace told. Spock concentrated on ignoring the stabbing pains in his hands. His fingers and palms were scraped raw, and the cold was making them ache more. He couldn't afford the time or effort necessary to set up mental blocks against the pain, so he endured it.

Zar was a little better off. His hands were hardened by years of exposure, and the cold didn't affect him. Hunger was another thing—the pangs in his middle were hard to ignore. Hunger in the past had always been a thing to fear, and his habitual reaction made it hard to concentrate his perceptions on sensing the enemy.

They had covered nearly half a kilometer of broken, rock-studded ground before they reached the perimeter of the screen and knew it had all been for nothing.

Whoever was commanding the Romulan task force was taking no more chances on unauthorized intrusion. Guards were paired and stationed in open areas just out of visual range of each other . . . *well within earshot*, Spock thought, taking out his phaser, only to look at it and put it away again. *Too much noise, even on stun. And the open areas make a sneak ambush impossible. . . .*

The Vulcan turned to his companion. "Do you think you could run fast enough to make it past them if I fired from cover?"

Zar shook his head. "Even if I thought I could, I wouldn't go under those conditions, If we both fired together . . ."

"Too much noise—the next pair would be on us in seconds. Frankly, I doubt I could outrun them, even with a head start. These are Romulans we're dealing with . . . not Humans. We have no advantage."

"How long . . ."

"Fourteen point four minutes."

They lay quietly, watching the soldiers as they stood, hands resting on the butts of their weapons. Spock felt the seconds ticking by in his head, and

153

bit his lip. Inexorably, the equation built itself in his mind, and the only logical outcome for any action they took at this moment was death. He found himself trying to reason whether death by phaser bolt was preferable to death by cataclysm when the planet was sliced apart—and shook his head, frustrated. There *must* be another alternative!

Zar narrowed his eyes, looking past the guards. Just beyond them he could see the distortion of the cloaking device. The sight tantalized him . . . safety, only a few meters away, and he was going to die within sight of it. In a very few minutes, now, lying here in the dust. He slithered backward until he could crouch behind a rock and peer at the enemy. Seconds ticked by in his head. *Gathering . . . building.* He was going to die. Those Romulans out there were killing him. He hated them. He was going to die, not long from now. *Stronger—building, gathering . . . . Die.* Like Dave and Juan . . . like the guard he'd killed. . . . *He could feel the death.* . . .

When he realized his companion was no longer beside him, the Vulcan wriggled back until he could see him. Zar was crouched, fingers digging at the rock, breathing in gasps, his upper lip beaded with sweat. "I'm going to die," the whisper reached the Vulcan like the rattle of ipanki leaves in the wind. "I'm frightened . . . I hate them . . . I'm going to die."

Spock was sickened, and at the same time, he felt an irrational impulse to comfort his son. He reached out a hand, shook his shoulder, gently. "Stop it, Zar."

"Shut up," Zar gasped, then ignored him. He mumbled again, a litany, "I'm scared. I hate them. I'm going to die . . . death . . ." His gaze fastened on the guards, eyes wide, glazing. "Die . . ." His body stiffened, then the hands clenched on the rock loosened, and he tumbled over bonelessly.

Shocked, Spock stared at him, then in reflex looked at the guards. They were sprawled, not moving.

Nightmare-slow, he scrambled over to the limp figure, touched the wrist. Nothing, He pulled his son's head into his lap, felt his throat—a flutter, very slight . . . His fingers went to the temples. Summoning his mind, he concentrated, finally picked up the kar-selan mind-activity. Secondary—weak, very weak. But there. He took a long breath.

Probing, reaching, calling. The name, over and over, for as ancient magic would have it, the name is the identity. Zar—Zar—Gateway faded, the rocks were gone. The pain in his hands erased. Zar—Finally . . . he . . . touched! **ZAR!**

His son stirred and moaned under his hands. "Quiet," he ordered. "You did it. Lie still for a second."

Spock drew another deep breath, closed his eyes momentarily. When he opened them, Zar was looking at him, gray eyes still clouded, unfocused.

"Can you move? The way is open, if we go quietly. We haven't much time."

The young man nodded, tried to speak, failed. Gathering himself, his teeth fastened on his lip, then he moved.

"Good . . . take it easy . . . come on . . . ." Spock put an arm under his shoulders, heaved. Zar's legs buckled for a second, then steadied. They stumbled, wavering, past the guards. Neither looked at the Romulans.

A short distance past the cloaking device perimeter, the younger man's natural resiliency began to return. He shook off the Vulcan's arm, and walked by himself. They had five minutes left.

Chapter XVI

Gateway was quiet, its winds hushed for once, as if in anticipation of its extinction. Kirk, using his distance lenses, surveyed the area for the fourth time, McCoy paced in a circle, counting seconds in his head, afraid to look at his chrono. Kirk scanned the area again, then took out his communicator, opened the hailing channel, heard the now-familiar crackle of distortion that had been his only answer for the past five hours. Five agonizing hours since he'd awakened, still tired, to find that there had been no word, no signal from Spock. Giving the horizon one last examination, he put his distance lenses away, opened another channel.

"Kirk to *Enterprise.*"

"*Enterprise.* Uhura here."

"Lieutenant, prepare to beam up the landing party. Order Mr. Scott to . . ." Something in the ruins of the archeologists' camp caught his eye. "Belay that. Beam up Doctor McCoy and the security team. I'll follow in a second. Tell Mr. Scott to stand by to initiate destruction sequence 10. Kirk out."

McCoy swung to face him, "Jim, I've got to stay—" the transporter beam caught him and he and the security personnel were gone.

The Captain walked a few paces toward the ruined building, and stooped to gather up the object that had attracted his attention. The satin gleam of polished wood, marred by a scratch and a broken string—but still in miraculously preserved condition—Doctor Vargas' Stradivarius. Kirk held it, remembering the evening when he'd heard its music, and tenderly wrapped it in a torn remnant of cloth. Holding the violin under his arm, he took out his communicator, hesitated, checked his chrono. *Two more minutes,* he promised himself. That was a minute over the deadline. He would fight the urge to extend it even further, he knew, when the two minutes were up. But he'd fought himself before, since he'd become Captain, and won.

Kirk spent the two minutes thinking about Spock, wondering what had happened. Incidents raced through his mind, flashed and were gone, like the winding patterns of a stream. *Spock . . . hanging upside down in that ridiculous tree, grinning . . . bending over his sensors . . . or a chessboard . . . "Fascinating" . . . a man of honor in two Universes . . . Spock . . . staggering toward him, smeared with ashy dust . . .*

Kirk's eyes widened, and he began to run.

"Where have you been? What kept you?" The Captain grabbed the Vulcan by the shoulders, shook him, then steadied him as he swayed. "You don't know how glad I am to—" he broke off, looking at Spock's companion, then hastily took his arm, supporting Zar as he staggered. Moving slowly, the three headed back toward the camp.

"I have to report failure, Captain. We were unable to trigger the force field. Unfortunately, they've landed one of their ships within a few meters of the Guardian—though they seem to be taking no notice of it. The Romulans returned before I had time to turn on the unit, and we were forced to hide while they searched the area."

Zar stumbled, lurched, pulling Kirk off balance. Bracing himself, the Captain lowered the younger man onto a large boulder, and took out his communicator. "Kirk to *Enterprise.*"

"*Enterprise.* Lieutenant Commander Scott."

"Scotty, I found them, alive. Three to beam up."

A pause instead of the expected assent. Then,

"There's been a bit o' trouble here, sir. We just picked them up on our scanners. Ten Romulan warships, comin' fast. They'll be in range in less than a minute, Captain. I've ordered the shields up. Shall I drop them t' beam you aboard?"

Kirk's voice was tight. "Under no circumstances drop those shields. Try to hold them off. Those Federation ships should be arriving any minute. Between you and the *Lexington* you ought to be all right. Were they able to fix the *Lexington*'s shields?"

"Aye, Captain. I just talked with Commodore Wesley. Don't worry, sir. We'll be fine. There isna' a ship built can hold a candle t' the *Enterprise* in a fight."

"I know, Scotty. Good luck. Signal me as soon as . . . when you can, Scotty."

"Scott out."

Kirk snapped his communicator shut with a decisive click. "That's it. we're stuck here, gentlemen. My ship up there, fighting, and I'm not with her. Ten to two isn't good odds."

Spock surveyed his Captain's grim expression, then said, "Lieutenant Commander Scott is a fine officer and a good tactician. No one knows the *Enterprise* better—except for you, Jim."

"I know. And you're right about Scotty. I suppose the situation could be worse—but frankly I can't think how."

The three sat silently for a moment, then Kirk straightened purposefully. "I brought some supplies. Are you hungry?"

"Water?" Zar said, taking an interest in the proceedings for the first time. They shared water and emergency rations in silence. Kirk watched the sky, as though imagining the battle that must be taking place thousands of kilometers away, in space.

"Captain," the Vulcan said suddenly. "As long as we *are* here, the only logical course of action is to return and trigger the force field. With three phasers, we stand a much better chance."

158

Kirk looked at him. "You mean three times zero doesn't still equal zero? It did while I was in school. If they're already alerted, they'll be waiting for us. It'll be suicide."

"You are correct, although somewhat flamboyant in your manner of expression, Captain. However, now that the Romulan fleet is in the area, we can't chance them having more sophisticated detection equipment than the landing craft have with them. If the battle goes against the two starships . . ."

"We'll be dead anyway. I see your point. If we can activate that force field, it could buy the Federation fleet extra time . . . which could make all the difference." The Captain stood up. "All right. You rested enough to start?"

"Yes," responded two voices. The First Officer glanced at Zar as they rose. The food and water had helped, but the younger man was still pale, and there were dark smudges beneath his eyes.

Kirk looked at both of them. "Which of you is going to figure the odds against us this time?"

Spock raised an eyebrow, and something glinted in the dark eyes. "This time, Captain, the odds against us are a mere three thousand, five hundred and seventy-nine point zero-four-five to one."

"Terrific. A regular cakewalk."

Two left eyebrows rose at Kirk's comment, Zar said it. "Cakewalk, Captain?"

Kirk groaned. "McCoy predicted that this was going to happen—I should've listened to him. Two of you is two too many. Come on, let's go."

Zar nodded. "I read a poem about this kind of situation a couple of weeks ago. It was called *Horatius at the—*" he sagged limply, eyes rolling back in his head. Spock released the nerve pinch, grabbed him as he fell. Swinging an arm under the younger man's knees, he picked him up easily.

Kirk watched the Vulcan knowingly, and a smile softened his mouth. "That raises the odds, Mr. Spock."

The Vulcan returned his friend's look, eyes level. "No, Jim. I calculated them that way from the beginning." Turning, he headed for the camp building. The Captain picked up the supplies and the cloth-wrapped violin, and followed him.

When he caught up, just outside the ruined camp, Kirk said, voice carefully casual, "I hope you realize how he's going to take this when he wakes up."

Spock nodded. "That's why I'm hurrying. I don't intend to be here when he regains consciousness. He must outweigh me by thirteen kilos."

Kirk grinned.

The Vulcan placed the unconscious form inside the wrecked structure, searched for a moment, then dropped a scorched blanket over him. The Captain placed his bundle beside the young man. "Hope he takes this with him when he beams up."

"What is it?"

"Doctor Vargas' violin. Does he still have his communicator?"

Stooping, Spock checked the pockets of the coverall. "Yes."

"Let's go, then."

The First Officer led them back along the same path he and Zar had come only a few minutes before. They crossed the perimeter screen at the same point, passing the two guards, still lying face down, Kirk gave them a quick glance, and whispered, as they stole along, "Stunned?"

Spock didn't look around, and his answer reached the Captain faintly. "Dead—I think."

"You?" Kirk avoided a large rock, dropped down beside the Vulcan to scan the ground in front of them.

"Zar."

The Captain whistled under his breath.

It took the Science Officer only five minutes to activate the force field unit. The two carefully hid the external evidence of the shield's presence, then turned back toward the perimeter. They had nearly reached it when they heard a shout. Kirk stopped. "They must've found those guards. I'm afraid we've had it, Mr. Spock. Feel like recalculating those odds?"

"I know a hiding place. This way, Captain."

If it hadn't been been for Kirk's uniform, they might have pulled it off again, A flash from a Romulan beamer caught the gold braid, and they were dragged from their cramped niche. Their captors wasted neither time nor speech—the two officers were bound, and escorted under heavy guard into the Romulan encampment.

It was a large camp, Kirk saw, concentrating on memorizing the layout. Nine plasta-tents set up in a rough circle, with what he speculated was a supply and ammunitions dump in the center. Two ships, one of them larger than the other, were located on the far side of the camp. The ship near the Guardian had been gone when they set up the force field—Kirk hoped that meant that the enemy remained unaware of the time portal.

A slap between the shoulders sent him stumbling into the largest of the plasta-tents, and another slap sent him crashing to the rock floor. He lay, face ground into the gritty surface, as his ankles were bound, then attached to the cords that confined his wrists. Raising his head by the simple expedient of a hand in his hair, one of the guards gagged him. From the scuffling sounds on his left, he deduced that Spock was receiving the same treatment. A blindfold followed the gag, and then the sound of receding footsteps. Some extra sense, however, told him that he and Spock were not alone—there must be a guard with them. *Somebody's taking no chances. . . .* Kirk thought.

He tugged at his bonds, abandoned the attempt immediately. Whoever had tied him was an expert, and had also taken the precaution of running a loop around his throat. Any struggle to release himself would strangle him. Deprived of sensory impres-

161

sions, he fought the urge to speculate on his fate—or his ship's. The *Enterprise* would be all right—he had to believe that, or he was licked before the fight even started.

After a short interval, he heard footsteps behind him again, then a hand dragged his head up. The blindfold was pulled down, and Kirk squinted, blinded by sudden light. There was a soft, indrawn breath, then a voice—somehow familiar?—"Untie him and remove his gag. Turn the Vulcan over and let him watch this."

A moment later he was free, rubbing at his wrists, eyes adjusting to the tent's light. He could see a figure in front of him, lean, with a narrow foxy face, and the insignia of a full Commander. Kirk blinked, narrowed his eyes. The quasi-familiar voice came again, "Don't you recognize me, Captain Kirk? I know you. The Romulan Empire has no love for you, and I even less. We have a personal score to settle. You destroyed my Commander's honor." He straightened and saluted formally. "Commander Tal, at your service."

The Romulan moved over and performed a second inspection on Spock. "Commander Spock. The Empire once issued a writ for your execution, on the charges of treason and sabotage. That writ has never been cancelled." Tal began to pace the length of the tent, talking. "Your capture is fortunate, for it seemed our mission here was going to fail. We haven't been able to locate the Federation installation on this planet—nothing but a group of weak antiquarians, digging in these endless ruins. Clever of the Federation, to mask a military secret in that fashion . . . but you betrayed yourselves when you assigned a full-time starship patrol." The Romulan Commander beckoned, and a burly Centurion moved to stand in front of Kirk, arms swinging loosely, deliberately, by his sides. Tal continued after a moment.

"Captain Kirk, I respect your intelligence. You

know that we are strong. We pride ourselves on being the military power that will rule this Galaxy—and soon. That is because we act, not out of cruelty, as do the Klingons, but out of efficiency. So. I say to you now, let us be efficient about this. You already know that I will have you killed if you do not tell me what the Federation is hiding here. Your death will be, needless to say, unpleasant. I'm sure you realize that is an understatement. Why not tell me now, and I promise on my honor as a soldier that I will see that you live. You may even be allowed to rejoin your people, with none the wiser, but I cannot guarantee that. But you will live, and you will still enjoy living. I'll give you two of your solar minutes to think about it."

Tal waited patiently. The silence dragged by, and then the Romulan spoke again. "Your decision, Captain?"

Kirk stared at him, muscles taut in anticipation. Tal nodded, not displeased, and signaled to the burly soldier. "Stay away from his head—I want him able to talk." The guard grunted an assent, clenching his fist. After the third blow, the Captain's knees buckled. He hung limply in the guard's hands, gasping, arms weakly trying to cradle the pain in his middle, until they dropped him to lie again on the floor. Tal shrugged, and the guards moved to untie the Vulcan's gag.

The Romulan's voice changed from its impersonal monotone, deepened, became colder. "Commander Spock, it would please me personally to see you receive the same, but I know the futility of that. Vulcans can block pain, and even destroy themselves rather than betray a secret. It is impossible for us to wrench from you what you do not wish to give—but perhaps you will decide to be reasonable. . . ." He glanced at Kirk, then back at the First Officer. "Tell us, and spare your Captain more of the same. Otherwise, he will die before your eyes, knowing that you could have saved him, if he would not save himself."

Spock stared stonily at the Romulan officer's left knee. Tal clenched his fist. "You have no loyalty at all, do you, Vulcan? You care no more for your Captain than you did for my Commander. . . ." His hand raised, trembled, then he shook his head. "I'll look forward to your dying." He paused, then resumed more calmly, "Tell me, which one of you killed my guard? Frankly, I doubt that the Captain would have the strength to overpower a trained Romulan—so it must have been you. What about the other two? If you tell me what kills that makes no noise and leaves no mark, I can at least try to intercede for you. . . ."

Silence.

"Very well, Tie them again." The Romulan guards busied themselves. When the two Federation officers were once again tied, gagged and blindfolded, Tal said, "I think that I have convinced you that we are in earnest here. I leave you to think about this: I will return in a short while, with a device that has been newly developed by our scientists—so newly developed that it hasn't been tried on a Human. There is, they tell me, a small chance that its effects will be permanent. The device is a neural exciter—one that can be adjusted to generate impulses to the nervous system. It is capable of generating degrees of sensation from a slight tickling to the pain felt by one who is being burned alive."

Tal poked Kirk with his foot. "The advantage to this device is that electric and submotor impulses cause the entire effect. The victim is never physically hurt at all. Although test animals and humanoid . . . volunteers . . . seemed to go mad a high percentage of the time. The device can be used again and again, with no lowering of efficiency. What you will feel, Captain, will cause you to tell me everything. There will be no end to the pain—not even in death, as there was for your scientists. I wish the *Glory Quest* had arrived in time for us to use it yesterday . . . there'd be no need for all of this now."

He paused, then said quietly, "You know your limits, Kirk. Even the bravest man has a breaking point—you *will* tell. The only question is when, and how much you can endure. Think about it."

Chapter XVII

The *Enterprise* was taking a beating. The Romulan ships surrounded and harried her, as they would a wounded lioness, taking care to stay out of range of her fangs. She'd destroyed two, and the *Lexington* had gotten another, but her starboard deflectors were gone. The next shot she took there would split her shining hide. Wesley was keeping the *Lexington* carefully positioned to cover her against a starboard assault, but his forward deflectors were in bad shape.

Chief Engineer Scott had wisely fought a running battle; depending on his ship's superior firepower and speed, he'd blasted and retreated, and swung back to fire again. The battle had ranged in a rough ellipse around Gateway, but the Romulans were wary now, and less quick to follow when the Federation ships sped away. They knew the Star Fleet vessels wouldn't go far.

Scott shifted uneasily in the command chair. He didn't like sitting here; never had. It was his duty, and he did it well, but his first love was the *Enterprise*. It was physical pain to feel her engines straining, hear the damage reports coming in.

"B-Deck reports an explosion caused by leakage of fumes into the bulkheads, Mr. Scott. Damage-repair unit notified."

Scotty nodded at Uhura, turned back to Ensign Chekov, who was manning Spock's sensors. "Any report on that one the *Lexington* winged during that last pass, lad?"

"Aye, sir. They seem to be vobbling. I think their

gyro system must be out. I'm also picking up some radiation leakage . . . could be the power pile, sir."

"Good. I doubt we'll have t' worry about that one again."

Sulu turned. "Mr. Scott, sir. They're beginning another circling maneuver."

The Chief Engineer switched his attention to the forward viewscreen. The six navigable Romulan ships were turning, forming themselves into a wedge. Scott was puzzled at first, then realized the purpose of the configuration. They intended to drive the point of the wedge between the *Enterprise* and the *Lexington*. Once separated, the two ships would be unable to compensate for each other's lost deflectors.

"Helm hard over t' starboard, zero four five point six, mark."

"Aye, Mr. Scott." Sulu's fingers flickered over his controls.

The *Lexington* was moving also, closing to port. The two vessels looked like massive, yet graceful dancers. They swung together, bobbing slightly as their aft deflector shields touched intermittently, repulsing each other with an aurora borealis shimmer. Scott smiled. "Good piloting, Mr. Sulu. Let' em try and drive us apart noo."

The enemy ships were still for a moment, then broke the wedge. They reformed into a rough circle, then suddenly split apart, heading for the two starships at maximum sublight speed. Three dived for the *Enterprise*'s port side, and three for the *Lexington*'s starboard side, phasers blossoming as they passed. The Federation ships were hampered from swinging their main phaser batteries toward the attackers by their proximity to each other. The *Enterprise* lurched under the impact of three direct hits; the *Lexington* took two.

Sulu turned, grim-faced. "That did it for our port screens, sir."

Scotty thought, drumming his fingers on the arm of the Captain's chair. "What would Jim Kirk do?"

he mumbled under his breath. Mentally he added, *Dinna rush, Scotty old lad. You're playing right into their hands, if you do. Take it slow . . . make 'em come t' us.* . . . His eyes narrowed at the thought, and he concentrated on the viewscreen.

The Romulans were circling again, but, like hunters when the prey begins to stagger, they hadn't withdrawn as far this time. Scott straightened. "Range, Mr. Sulu?"

"40,000 kilometers, sir."

"Arm all photon torpedoes. Shut down the power in the forward phaser bank t' half-capacity. Shut it down altogether in the port banks. When they scan us, they'll think the damage caused an overload." *At least I hope they will,* he added silently.

The helmsman turned back a moment later. "Photon torpedoes armed and tracking, Mr. Scott."

"Aye, Mr. Sulu. We'll just wait for 'em. Right noo, they're thinkin' somethin' like, 'Noo how bad did we hurt 'em?' We'll give 'em their answer in a moment. Lieutenant Uhura, are you getting anything from the *Lexington?*"

"Yes, Mr. Scott. Their photon torpedoes armed and tracking, also. They report starboard and forward deflectors lost on that last run."

They waited. Finally the Romulan ships began to edge closer, almost drifting under short bursts of impulse power.

"Range, Mr. Sulu?"

"Thirty-five thousand kilometers, Mister Scott— and closing, sir."

"Keep trackin' 'em, Mister."

"Aye, sir."

Scott shut his eyes and counted three, slowly. Then, "Fire, Mr. Sulu."

The helmsman's hand flashed across his board. The *Enterprise* quivered slightly as each bank of torpedoes launched. Nobody breathed.

Suddenly the viewscreen was illuminated by a brilliant white light. The bridge crew whooped briefly. Scott turned to Chekov. "Status, lad?"

"Ve got one, sir! And the *Lexington* got annoder— I think the *Lexington* scored a second hit, but no measurable damage on that sheep."

The Chief Engineer slumped back, watching the four remaining enemy ships wearily. *It isna' going t' be enough*, he thought. *We've really pulled their teeth, but it's still two t' four, and we're hurt.* He fancied that he could hear his ship panting, and silently apologized to her. *Good try, lass, but . . .*

Uhura turned toward him, her voice jubilant. "Mr. Scott! We're being hailed, sir!"

Chekov was gesturing wildly at the scanners. "Sheeps, sir! Five of them! Just entering this sector!"

Chapter XVIII

Zar was dreaming of death, and pain. The dream
spun and dissolved into each other, leaving no memory behind:

> He was sliding in frantic haste, knowing that
> it made no difference, the rope scoring his
> hands—and there was her body, hair flung fan-
> wise over the ice, almost covering the unnatural
> angle of the neck. . . .
> He threw his arm over his throat as the vitha
> sprang, and felt the rip of the fangs. . . .
> Juan and Dave, torn bits of humanity, seen
> through McCoy's mind . . .
> The queer blankness—had it been dark, or
> light?—of that place—(where?). He'd been there
> after projecting his own death at the Romulan
> guards, when that summoning had come, drag-
> ging him back. The bond he couldn't ignore,
> whether or not he wished to—calling, with des-
> perate force of will—calling . . .

His eyes opened on darkness. The dream was gone
leaving nothing but that sense of—what?

Memory rushed back. They'd been in the ruins
ready to go back to the time portal, and then he wa
here. He moved cautiously, felt the known ache o
bruised nerves in his shoulder and realized what ha
happened. As he moved, the pain in his shoulde

170

lanced upward to his head and down into his middle. Nausea gagged him as he held his head with both hands, half-convinced it would roll off his shoulders if he didn't

"No . . ." His own agonized whisper startled him. *"Not again.* Please . . ." At the moment, even his own death seemed preferable to that involuntary sharing of another's.

Anger saved him. When he concentrated on the anger and the shame of being left behind, the sickness was blotted out. Mentally, he built a pyre, heaped it high with every cold look, every withdrawal, every negative word; then torched it with that nerve pinch. The anger-flames were comforting, warming, driving out the sickness.

Just as he reached a fever pitch of rage, though, something happened. It was like looking at one of those pictures Jan Sajii had, the kind where there were two outlines, but you could only see one at a time. The black and the white images—and somehow, as you stared, by some trick, there would be a whole new image fronting you. He fingered the blanket that had been pulled over him, and McCoy's words echoed, *"Illogical as it may seem, all fathers tend to be over-protective. . . ."*

Anger was gone, burned away by understanding, and somehow Zar knew the reason behind that nerve pinch, understood Spock as he never had before, and a strange, sad pride grew out of that comprehension. The Vulcan had chosen to leave *him* behind—although the emotion Zar sensed his father felt for Kirk was strong, Kirk was not here, *he* was.

When he was able to move, he stumbled out of the wrecked building, unable to endure the stink of death, and sat down on a boulder to think—to plan. They'd been captured, or were in immediate danger of some sort, but at the moment, were still alive. (Somehow he was sure that if Spock died, he'd *know*, apart from the concern he felt for the Captain.) Assuming that they were still alive, then the Romulan camp was the place to look first.

He searched his pockets, found the phaser and his communicator. Having never used one before, he fumbled for a moment, but finally opened the channel, cleared his throat.

"Enterprise? Lieutenant Uhura?"

A crackle of static, then a startled contralto. "Zar! Wait until I scramble!" The voice faded out, was replaced after a brief interval by another.

"Lad, is that you? Where are the captain and Mr. Spock?"

"Scotty, they've been captured, I think. We need to go after them, *now*. They're in danger." Zar winced as pain flashed behind his temples.

"But the cloakin' device is still up, lad. We canna send the landin' party in blind. And how do ye know they're in danger? Did you escape?"

"I didn't go with them." Zar bit his lip, frustrated, then remembered something. "Ask Doctor McCoy, he'll tell you that I know what I'm talking about. And I can get the landing party into the camp without being seen. *Ask McCoy.*"

After a short pause he heard the Scottish burr again. "All right, lad. I canna' leave myself, but I'll send down a party. They'll be joinin' you directly."

Zar remembered something. "Is Doctor McCoy still there?"

"Yes, I'm here. What is it?" The Doctor sounded impatient.

"There's a bundle in the left-hand cabinet in my quarters. I'll be needing it. Can you send it down?"

"Send it? Hell, I'll *bring* it. I'm not sitting up here biting my nails one minute longer. McCoy out."

Zar closed the channel with relief, and waited for the others.

The party was made up of six security people and Doctor McCoy, with Lieutenant Uhura commanding.

"How are things aboard the *Enterprise?*" was Zar's

172

first question, as he munched on an emergency rations wafer from Uhura's supplies.

"We'd thought we'd had it for sure, then the Admiral and the other four ships showed up." Uhura replied, "We sustained a few injuries, but fortunately no deaths in the battle. The Romulan ships self-destructed immediately—we didn't take any prisoners."

"I wonder if the Romulan forces here know about the outcome of the fight?" Phillips, one of the security force spoke up, methodically checking the extra charge for her phaser. "If they do, they'll be massed against us."

"Unless their communications equipment is specially geared to penetrate that energy barrier, they *can't* know," Uhura said. "That cloaking device sets up bands of interference as bad as seli-irinium shielding. I wasn't able to pick up any transmissions directed at the camp from the enemy ships, either."

"Good." Zar took a swallow of water. "Then our first move should be to get inside the perimeter again, and locate the Captain and Mr. Spock. I can find them . . . I think." He frowned slightly, rubbed futilely at the dirt on his face with an equally filthy hand. "But once we locate them, how do we get them out of the camp?"

"We don't have the force for a direct assault," Uhura said thoughtfully, drawing patterns in the dust with a long fingernail. "Some sort of diversion would be our best answer. Preferably one that would destroy the cloaking device at the same time. That way, we could call for reinforcements afterward."

"Do you have any idea what it looks like?" Zar asked.

Uhura shook her head. "I saw the one we stole from the Romulans several years ago, but there's no guarantee this one will resemble it. But there's one thing . . ." The fingernail tapped against a rock as she considered, "It's bound to be large. Possibly too

173

large to move easily. There's a good chance it's mounted in the landing craft."

Zar nodded and stood up. "That gives us something to go on, then. And destroying their shuttle even without the cloaking device in it, should be enough to cause our diversion. Let's go."

Zar led them back inside the perimeter at a steady dogtrot, assuring them that there were no Romulans around.

"They must believe their fleet destroyed or captured the Federation forces, and that they're safe," McCoy said, puffing a little as they crouched in the lee of a tumbled wall. "Or else they think we wouldn't dare mount an offensive as long as they hold Jim and Spock prisoner. Still, I don't like it. They may just be playing cat-and-mouse."

Slanted brows drew together in a frown, and the gray eyes were puzzled. "Cat-and-mouse? Another game like poker?" Zar hazarded.

"Sort of," Uhura smiled, then lowered her voice. "We can only keep going. Where is the Guardian in relation to here?"

"About 60 meters that way," the young man said, pointing. "I brought us through the screen in a different area. I didn't think you'd want the others to see it, since the Captain said it was a secret."

"Right." Uhura bit her lip. "Still, we should check and see if the force field has been activated. Doctor, you stay with the others, here. Zar and I will check the shielding."

The two were back in a few minutes. "They got that far, anyway," Uhura said, relieved. "Now for the camp."

The rescue party surveyed the Romulan forces from the shelter of a broken pavement that was located on a slight rise. "Nine tents, and a supply dump," Chu Wong, the ranking security officer whispered thoughtfully, his dark eyes narrowed even more than usual. "I'd estimate a force of about 80."

Uhura was looking at the two shuttles positioned

side by side directly across the camp from them. "Probably less, Lieutenant," she said, "unless they transported down another group and sent the other shuttle back."

McCoy looked over at Zar, who was staring straight ahead, gray eyes unfocused. "Which tent are they in, son?"

The younger man shivered, then blinked and his gaze cleared. "That one," he said confidently, "the third from the left end."

"Are they both there?" McCoy asked.

"Yes," Zar nodded. He'd picked up the Captain's emotional emanations easily, even though they were subdued, edged with pain. Spock's presence had been harder to sense, but he'd finally caught the concern, the continually logical evaluation of the situation. And pain, though masked, unacknowledged.

"They must be under restraints," Zar breathed, "and the Captain is barely conscious. I think he's hurt. They're alone."

"All right," Uhura thought for a moment. "Zar, if you can cause that diversion, we'll take care of the Captain and Mr. Spock. Do you think you can get in there and out without being seen?"

Zar hefted his phaser and a faint smile bracketed the normally sober mouth, "Easily," he said, and McCoy had seen that touch of arrogance on another face. "Give me ten minutes, and then be ready to move—fast. You'll know when." With a hiss of fabric against stone, he was gone.

Spock lay on the rock floor, feeling the cold seep upward into his body. In one way it was a blessing, for it numbed the pain of twisted arms and legs, of bonds pulled too tight, of the gag that made it agony to breathe. In another way, the cold itself was torture for him, he who felt perpetually chilled in temperatures humans regarded as comfortable. He closed his eyes, summoning strength, bringing the vedra prah controls into play, forcing his mind to acceptance of the discomfort, then negation of it. He was successful, to an extent, but the effort ate further into his physical reserves. Exhaustion was close, and when it set in . . .

How much time had passed? Fatigue dulled his time sense, but yielded to disciplined concentration—twenty minutes and thirty seconds since Tal's departure. One hour and fourteen minutes exactly since their capture. And how many minutes until their deaths? He listened to the breathing beside him—regular, shallow—the Captain was either asleep, or unconscious. The Vulcan wished that he'd been able to leave Jim behind, too. He had no personal fear of death—it was simply a lack of biological existence, with either something or nothing following—but the thought of Kirk's death was a pain that mind-control could not block.

Time—how much time did they have left? By now, Zar should have awakened, contacted the ship—he felt a stab of concern for the *Enterprise*—perhaps help was on the way? Reason overcame hope. It was unlikely—involuntarily his mind computed the odds—that anyone from the ship would know they'd been captured. Nobody would know of their deaths. . . .

No. As the thought occurred, he knew it for error. One person would know, he was sure of it, despite all logic. Zar would feel their deaths, *his* death, through the bond, that link that was no longer something that could be accepted or denied, but existed a fact, and therefore inarguable. *Forged in mind, tempered in blood*—the ancient Vulcan phrase ran through his mind, followed by its Human analogue—*bone of my bone, flesh of my flesh.* . . .

He felt intense regret that Zar would be a helpless partner to his demise, but could think of no way to avert it. Hopefully, the Romulans would be quick—for both of them.

Kirk roused from a cramped half-doze, wincing as his ribs stabbed fire against the cold of the rocky floor. As his mind cleared, he began rubbing his jaw hard on the gritty rock beneath his cheek. He heard another swishing noise, realized Spock was doing the same.

Both sides of his face were raw fire, but the gag slipped. He spit it out, worked his mouth to get the jaw muscles moving again, swallowed a fraction of the cottony dryness, "Spock?"

A grunted assent from the Vulcan, then the quiet voice, "Captain—are you hurt badly? You've been unconscious for some time—ever since Tal left. . . ."

Kirk made an impatient sound. "Never mind that. If they untie both of us, you know what to do if you get the chance." He waited for agreement, heard none. "Damn it, Spock, that's an order. I'll do it myself if I get the opportunity. . . ." He turned his head toward the First Officer, ignoring the slowly tightening loop around his neck—and then realized what a fool he'd been. Deliberately, he began thrashing, feeling the noose tighten, holding his breath against the pain in his ribs and throat.

"Jim, no!"

The Vulcan moved, ignoring the jerk of the noose on his own throat, vainly trying to reach that gasping figure whose struggles were fast weakening. Then, behind him, he heard the opening of the tent, and a muffled exclamation—Tal's voice. "Kirk, no!" Feet stumbled over the Vulcan's legs as the Romulan flung himself between them.

Spock could hear the rasp of a blade against the cords, and knew that the Romulan Officer was cutting the Captain's bonds. He strained sensitive ears, and was rewarded by a faint gasp—Kirk wasn't—

The ground beneath them rocked, and the Commander pitched between the two prisoners with the force of the explosion. Shards of rock and debris spattered against the tough outside of the tent, and gradually the shock waves died down. Tal scrambled to his feet, shouting orders and inquiries, and rushed

177

out of the tent, leaving the two Federation officers alone.

Outside, Spock could hear shouts, orders, and running feet. Inside, there were only those wheezing breaths. He called his Captain's name repeatedly, but Kirk was either unconscious or unable to talk. He stopped in the middle of one cautious inquiry to listen—heard a rip at the back of the tent, and then a voice. *Uhura's? Impossible. . . .*

But it was. "Thank heaven we found you, sir." Gentle hands that nevertheless moved with sure strength severed his bonds, and the Vulcan sat up, blinking, as he pushed the blindfold off. Even in the dim light of the tent, it was hard to make out the Lieutenant's features—his eyes watered after the total blackness.

"The Captain—" he began, and heard McCoy's reassuring mutter.

"Jim's all right—well, depends on your definition. Shock, exhaustion, three broken ribs . . . he should be in sickbay. But if I know him, he'll want to—" The Vulcan could hear several shots from the hypo hiss, then McCoy's grumble again, ". . . the worst patient in Star Fleet, won't rest, has to do it all himself, you watch—"

By this time Spock could see, watched as the Doctor, never ceasing his monologue, deftly bound Kirk's rib cage in an elastic bandage that automatically adjusted for maximum support. By the time McCoy had finished, Kirk was conscious.

"Bones . . . Uhura . . . I'm glad to see you. How'd you get here?" His hazel gaze turned to the Vulcan and narrowed in puzzlement. "Seems to me that there was an explosion—or was that just the one in my head? There were a lot of them. . . ." He winced as he took a deep breath.

"No, Jim," McCoy said. "That was Zar. We sent him off to create a diversion, and he blew both Romulan craft sky-high. He must've overloaded his phaser.

178

"Is he all right?" Something in the Vulcan's voice made the three of them turn to face him.

"We haven't seen him, sir." Uhura said. "I presume he got out of the blast area. Come on, we'd better get out of here—if you can walk, Captain."

"I'm fine." Kirk's face belied his words as he stood, and he didn't refuse the supporting arms offered him by the Doctor and his First Officer.

Once outside the camp, Uhura hailed the *Enterprise*.

"Enterprise, Scott here."

Uhura handed the communicator to Kirk. "Scotty, this is the Captain. What's your status?"

"Repairs are underway, sir, but in general, we were fortunate. No deaths, a few injuries, only one serious. McCoy can tell you better aboot them. Admiral Komack has been callin' and he's on the other channel right noo. The cloakin' device is gone, sir." He paused, then continued, "Admiral Komack says he monitored an explosion down there."

"Yes. Patch me in to him, Scotty."

As Kirk talked to the Admiral, Spock, McCoy and Uhura turned to survey the remains of the Romulan camp. The blast had leveled several of the tents closest to the wrecked shuttles, and there was turmoil and disorder everywhere. As they watched, a party of Federation marines trotted through the center of the camp, heavy-duty phasers cradled at ready. In the distance they could hear the occasional whine of phasers set for maximum stun.

"Not *Enterprise* security." McCoy observed.

"I would speculate that Admiral Komack dispatched them, as soon as the cloaking device was removed, Doctor," Spock said, never turning from his constant scanning of the tumbled figures near the blast area. McCoy suddenly realized who the Vulcan was looking for, and in unspoken agreement, the two walked back into the camp. The only casualties however, wore Romulan uniforms. They picked their way among them, and McCoy occasionally dropped to

179

check a prone figure, then summoned Federation medical personnel if the Romulan was still alive.

"Actually, they're as lucky as we are," the Doctor said, after they finished their grim check. "It could have been worse. That blast was nearly contained by the bulk of the two ships. It was set carefully—to destroy as few—"

"Bones, Spock!" They turned, to find Kirk picking his way toward them. "The Admiral reports that our forces are nearly in complete control. I've put Uhura in charge of supervising the prisoners. Chu Wong and his people are assisting the mop-up squad."

"Good." McCoy said decisively. "That means that Spock can stay here to look for Zar, and I can get you back to sickbay before you collapse. Admiral Komack's got the situation in hand."

"Not so fast, Bones. You've forgotten one thing. As long as this planet's swarming with unauthorized personnel, we'll need a constant watch on the Guardian. The three of us have been detailed to that until all Federation and Romulan forces have been transported off the surface. Come on."

Despite Kirk's protests that he was fine, the way back to the time portal was a slow one. Several times the Captain was forced to rest, ignoring McCoy's protests that he should beam back to the *Enterprise* and leave the others to guard the time portal.

Finally, they sighted the monolithic form. As they moved haltingly toward it, McCoy narrowed his eyes, then touched Spock's arm. The Vulcan had already seen the ashy dust puffing up from the opposite side of the portal. A moment later, sounds of a scuffle reached them. Spock and McCoy broke into a run, and Kirk, teeth fastened in his lip, quickened his limping hobble.

The two officers rounded the temple wall and saw twin dark figures rolling in the dust, loud gasps punctuated by grunts of pain as they groped for each other's throats. To McCoy's suprise, both wore Romulan uniforms, and he wondered briefly what

180

they were fighting over before his vision cleared and he recognized Zar's features under streaks of blood and smeared dust.

Spock's voice rang loud, cutting through the agonized sounds of the combat. "Tal, drop the weapon. *Now.*"

Chapter XIX

At the sound of Spock's voice, the thrashing intensified until the onlookers could barely see for the choking dust. The Doctor heard his own voice, tight with anxiety. "Spock, your phaser! Stun Tal!" From out of the melee on the ground, a hand—Tal's hand, they could tell by the Romulan insignia— reached, groped, then closed on the Romulan sidearm that had been knocked to the side. Zar evidently saw the barrel of the weapon turning toward his head, and heaved wildly at the Romulan's body. Spock hesitated, trying for a clear shot.

McCoy flung himself at the Vulcan's weapon. "Stun *both* of them, for God's sake! He's going to kill Zar!" Out of the corner of his eye, he saw the younger man's knee move, heard Tal's grunt, then his fingers closed around the phaser and McCoy turned to fire.

Spock shoved the Doctor's hand, spoiling his aim, just as they saw the flash of a blade in Zar's hand. They heard the muffled impact as it connected with the back of Tal's neck, and then the Romulan sagged, limp.

Zar let him sprawl in the dust as he pulled himself to a kneeling position, leaning heavily on a nearby boulder. The young man's breathing was a ragged sob . . . the only sound in the stillness.

McCoy moved to the Romulan and turned him over, then stared in surprise as his hands came away unstained. Kirk joined him, and both men looked up at Zar's words to Spock—formal, almost ritualistic.

"Just as I have shadowed thy life, thy shadow now lies over me." Zar straightened, his mouth a grim slash. "I hit him with the butt . . . *not* the blade."

Tal gasped, moaned, and McCoy hastily took out a charge for his hypo, pressed it into the Commander's shoulder. The Romulan sagged again. "That should hold him, Bones," Kirk said. "We'll take him with us when we beam up."

"How did you find him, Zar?" asked the Doctor, standing up. "And where did you get the uniform?"

"I came back here to make sure nobody would tamper with the Guardian." Zar replied. "Then I saw him, digging around the unit we installed. I was able to get close enough wearing the uniform to jump him. I 'borrowed' the uniform from one of the sentries before I planted my phaser to overload."

"And to think we didn't want you to come with us because Spock was worried you'd get hurt." Kirk lowered himself gingerly onto a fallen column, shaking his head. "Tell me, have you ever considered joining Star Fleet? We could use someone with talents like yours."

Zar started to say something, then bit his lip. As they watched, his expression changed, became shadowed, remote. "I'm afraid not, Captain." He turned to McCoy. "Did you bring along that duffle bag from my quarters I mentioned?"

McCoy pointed. "Over there. What's in it, anyhow?"

"Clothes." Zar said shortly, stooping to pick up the bundle, then continuing out of sight behind a large boulder.

The Doctor looked puzzled, then glanced back at the time portal, quiescent, grimly lifeless. "Helluva lot of trouble over a big stone doughnut, wasn't it, Jim?"

Kirk nodded, an echo of old sadness in his voice, "But still worth it, Bones. Always worth it."

It was Spock who saw Zar return from changing

his clothes, and the other officers turned at his indrawn breath.

The leather tunic was tight, now, and the rough breeches pulled taut around hard-muscled legs above the fur mukluks. Only the gray fur cloak, sweeping the ground, fit the same as it had seven weeks ago. Zar stooped, gathered up the hide bag that contained his few possessions from the past, and slung it across his back, fastened it with thongs. Then he faced them, head up, his expression calm but watchful.

Spock was the first of them to find his voice, and it was incongruously normal-sounding. "You are going back?"

"Yes." The remoteness faded he met Spock's eyes, watched his father get up, walk over to face him. *"I have to.* We've all risked our lives to make sure history isn't changed, and I have reason to believe it will be if I don't return. I'm needed there . . ." His mouth softened into what was almost a wry smile. "Needed there, as I'd never be here—despite the Captain's kind remark. McCoy *was* right. Two of us *is* two too many. I don't want to spend my life trying to stay out of your shadow. . . . And I would. So I'm leaving. What better place to go than a planet where my skills, what I have to offer . . . teach . . . are needed desperately?" His voice softened. "After all, it's my home."

"What makes you think you'll change history if you don't return? Living in that arctic wilderness alone—" Spock half-protested.

"I'm not going to be alone. Instead of the Northern hemisphere of Sarpeidon, I'm going to the Southern one . . . to the Lakreo Valley." Zar watched recognition dawn in Spock's eyes as he mentioned his destination.

"The Lakreo Valley 5,000 years ago?" Kirk frowned. "I . . . what's the significance of that?"

"Ask Mr. Sp—" Zar hesitiated and his shoulders straightened even more. "Ask my father. I can tell he remembers."

"The Lakreo Valley . . . the Sarpeidon equivalent of the Tigris-Euphrates civilization on Earth . . . or the Khal at R'sev on Vulcan. A remarkable cultural awakening. Within a comparatively short span of time, the backward hunting and gathering tribesmen developed many of the basics of civilization. A spoken and written language—the zero—agriculture—" The Vulcan's dry recitation paused, and Zar took up the list, eyes shining.

"Domestication of animals—smelting metal—architecture. More than that. All within a *very* short span of time. An unprecedented development in a people's history. Such rapid growth logically indicates that they had help. I have strong evidence to indicate that help was me."

"But Beta Niobe . . ." McCoy began, and stopped. Zar nodded gravely.

"Oh, it will still blow up. But my people will have had 5,000 years of civilization that they might not otherwise have. Five thousand years is a respectable time span for anyone—especially when you think about the fact that the culture didn't die. It's all there, the important things, in the computer banks of the Federation, where we both saw them." He took a deep breath. "I *know* this is what I must do—without me, there won't be any cultural awakening. Or maybe a different one, and that would change history."

Some of the tension in the air eased suddenly as Zar's teeth flashed in a wry grin. "The entire notion sounds incredibly arrogant when I hear it out loud."

McCoy cleared his throat gruffly. "I wouldn't worry about it. You come by it honestly." He watched a suggestion of that same smile soften the Vulcan's hard mouth for a second at his words, and wasn't sure he'd seen it until Spock nodded.

"I first realized the truth the other day, just before the landing party died. I was studying the tapes Spock had been looking at, plus some others I found in the library. Things started to add up." He shrugged one shoulder in the old self-deprecating way. "Hadn't

185

any of you ever wondered *why* my mother spoke English?"

Zar started to turn away, toward the time portal. Spock's voice stopped him. "Wait." The Vulcan cleared his throat, and his words were soft, but perfectly distinct. "I have been . . . planning. Thinking. Before you mentioned leaving, that is. I would like you to accompany me to Vulcan, to meet . . . the Family. Are you sure you must go?"

Zar nodded without speaking.

Spock took a deep breath. "You must do what you have decided is right, then. But first . . ." He moved toward the younger man, stretching out his hand, fingers reaching for his head. Zar stiffened, then relaxed visibly as the older man's lean fingertips pressed lightly between the slanting brows so like the Vulcan's own. The two stood, eyes closed, for long moments.

Kirk had never seen two telepaths mind-meld, and hadn't realized that the tension-filled contact points of spread fingers weren't necessary. This contact was quiet, undramatic, almost gentle. Finally Spock dropped his hand, and weariness seemed to settle over him like a cloak.

Zar's eyes opened and he took a deep breath, blinking. "The meld . . ." He was clearly shaken. "The truth . . . is a great gift. . . ."

"No one has a greater right to know." Spock's voice was deeper than usual, and the expression in his eyes mirrored the warmth in Zar's.

The younger man turned away after a moment, moved to clasp hands with Kirk. "Captain, it would be better if they think I died—in the explosion, or the fight with Tal. Nobody has to know I used the time portal." He looked over at the gigantic rocky oval. "I have a feeling that nobody will ever be allowed to use it again. We came too close to disaster this time."

"Admiral Komack seemed to be thinking along those same lines, so you're probably right, Zar. Yo know that means you can't change your mind. Besides, there's no portal on the other side. Are you sure you want to do this?"

"I'm sure, Captain. This is the right thing for me."

"I wish you luck, then. How will the Guardian know where to put you?"

"It will know." Zar sounded so confident that Kirk didn't argue with him. They shook hands again, and the younger man frowned. "One thing worries me, Captain. Will you get in trouble for breaking General Order Nine?"

Kirk chuckled weakly, then stopped as his ribs protested. "It's been logged that you volunteered, and you're an adult. Under the circumstances, I suppose they'll have to overlook it. After all, you did save the whole show."

Zar raised an eyebrow. "I had *some* help, Captain. . . ." The laughter in the gray eyes died, as he leaned close and whispered, "Take care of him, please."

Kirk nodded.

McCoy's voice was gruff as they shook hands. "Take care of yourself, son. Remember, never draw from an inside straight."

"I'll remember. I'll have to teach my people how to play poker, though, before I'll get a chance to put all you taught me into practice. But think of the advantage I'll have!" The gray eyes belied the light words. "I'll miss you. You know, indirectly, you're to blame for my decision."

"I am?"

"Yes. You were the one who told me to grow up. And I knew when I saw those history pages that it wasn't going to be easy. But I'm trying."

"You're doing fine." McCoy took a deep breath, tried to smile.

Zar walked over to the Guardian, reached down and removed the last wire from the force field unit. Straightening, he looked at Spock, and voiced a phrase in Vulcan. The other replied briefly in the same language. Turning, Zar placed a hand on the blue-gray rock and stood silently, head bowed, for a long moment.

The time portal did not speak this time. Instead of the usual vapor and swirling images, one picture sprang sharp and clear into its middle, holding steady. They could see mountains in the distance, and blue rivers running through meadows of the mossy aqua grass. Beta Niobe, no longer so angry-looking, was high, and they knew it was summer.

Zar turned his head, addressed Spock one last time. "I leave you my pictures, past and future, as a symbol." Then he leaped, graceful as a cat, through the portal.

They saw him land, watched him pull off his cloak and shake his head in the warmth, saw his nostrils expand as he sniffed the air. Kirk wondered if the younger man could see them, and thought that he probably couldn't—then there was a movement at his elbow. Spock, eyes fixed, was walking toward the Guardian. One step, two, three . . .

And then Kirk, moving with a jerk that stabbed his ribs, caught his arm, his voice low, desperate. *"Spock. He doesn't need you."* And he wondered if the Vulcan caught the unvoiced addition, *And I . . . we . . . do.*

As they stood poised, the Vulcan's motion halted, suspended, the image flicked out forever.

Epilogue

"Night" aboard the huge starship. The lights were dimmed, the corridors quiet. Occasional crew members, returning to their quarters after late duty, or reporting for the early morning shift, moved soft-footed. Even the turbo-lift seemed hushed as Kirk left its small interior for the deck. He moved quietly to a door, hesitated, then flashed the signal. "Come," said a voice from within almost immediately.

As he'd suspected, the Vulcan hadn't gone to bed. He was sitting at his deck, his micro-reader still on. Kirk sat down at his nod. "Greetings, Captain."

"Greetings, Mr. Spock. Thought I'd drop by and see how you were doing." He stretched cautiously, still favoring his healing ribs. "Rough day."

"Agreed." The Vulcan's eyes were hooded with fatigue, but shone with a tiny spark in their dark depths. "The memorial service you conducted today was . . . most fitting, Captain. I am sure the families of the archeologists as well as the crew would find it so."

Kirk sighed. "The only thing that made it bearable was the knowledge that one of the names on that roster didn't belong there. Or did it? I'm not sure I know how to remember him. As someone alive, just on the other side of the centuries, or as someone who . . . died . . . 5,000 years ago." Spock didn't reply; his gaze was fixed again on the screen in front of him.

"Did you notice how many friends he'd made, just in the short time he was with us, Spock? Christine Chapel, Uhura, Scotty, Sulu . . . even some crew I didn't recognize. That young Ensign—what's her name?"

"McNair. Teresa McNair."

"I wish I could tell them the truth. That would make it so much easier. Are those his paintings?" Kirk walked over to the canvases stacked against the screen, began, after a nod from the Vulcan, to look through them.

"Yes." Spock said, watching him. "I thought I would give some of them to his friends. I believe they would like that. A gift, in lieu of the truth they cannot know."

"That would be very generous, and I know it would mean a lot to them." Kirk bit his lip, gazing abstractedly at the last painting, then balled his fist suddenly and thumped it softly against the bulkhead. "Dammit! If only we were *sure* he made it! Doesn't that bother you, Spock? Wondering?"

The Vulcan was looking at him with that spark again in his eyes, and Kirk heard exultation, triumph, in the normally flat voice. "He made it, Captain. I have my proof."

Long fingers switched on the micro-reader, as Kirk walked over to the desk. "He left his pictures to me, remember? His pictures past *and future,* he said. Here it is, Jim. The symbol he found, the one that told him he had to go back. Here."

Kirk looked into the reader, saw the image on the screen. One part of his mind automatically read the caption, something about "a frieze from a palace wall in the trade city of New Araen . . . believed to have some esoteric religious significance . . ." but his eyes were so filled with the picture that the words made little sense. They didn't need to.

Against a dark background, white-flecked, loomed the familiar shape, the streamlined shapes of the power nacells surmounting the huge disk, somewhat distorted, but still unmistakable—caught in her passage through space.

The ship, and beneath it a hand, open-palmed, the fingers spanning time and distance in the Vulcan salute.

About the Author

Ann Crispin, 33, was born in Connecticut and has lived primarily in Maryland, near Washington, D.C. She received a B.A. in English from the University of Maryland in 1972. She is employed by the United States Census Bureau, and in her eight years there has held a number of positions, mostly as a writer and trainer about census data. Her former occupations include: training horses, managing swimming pools, teaching writing and horseback riding, processing mortgage loans, and selling lamps (no Genies, unfortunately).

Ann is married, she has a three-year-old son, two horses, three cats, and an eleven-percent mortgage (the acquisition of which she considers one of her major accomplishments). A lifelong Star Trek fan, her hobbies are reading, horseback riding, and attending science fiction conventions. She has just sold a second, non-Star Trek sf novel entitled *Suncastle*.